HOW LOVE CHANGED IT ALL

CHILDHOOD FRIEND'S GREW UP TO FALL IN LOVE AFTER SEARCHING FOR LOVE FOR YEARS

This is a work of fiction. Names, character, places and incidents are either the product of the author's imagination or are used fictitiously, and any resemblance to actual persons, living or dead, business establishments, events or locales is entirely coincidental.

@ COPYRIGHT 2022 BY (CHRISTOPHER WOODWARD)

CHAPTER 1

Texas Plano. I say it right away, along with the fact that it's January, so you can image a chilly, dreary environment at the beginning of the year. I would boast about being from Plano once springtime arrived, but at that moment, I would have given everything to be somewhere warm and lush. Now let's focus on a smaller area. On the northern side of one of the loops of Yellow Breeches, on Fortuna Lane, I reside. Depending on where and what you read, there might be a river or a creek. I've been told it's a top-notch stream for trout fishing, but since I don't fish, I'll have to take their word for it. Oh, and in case it matters, I'm located just west of the Summer River.First of all, we all grew up in Plano, and thanks to PTA mothers, we were all acquainted as children. In our little company, there were still the four of us after several went.In that small, close-knit group of four, my name is James Kent. The second male in our group is Austin Mark. Austin has sandy, almost red, hair that is often a mess. His hair doesn't care, not because he doesn't, so it spreads out in all directions. His most current remedy is to keep it extremely brief. Although he appears to be rather easy back, his mind is constantly active. I don't know how to characterize Angela Boston. What comes to mind is how vibrant she is. Energy-filled and frequently just on the verge of mischief. She can be impetuous, but she never gets out of control, and in my opinion, that simply adds to her attractiveness. I would constantly find justifications to touch her lovely brown hair, which she wore in a bouncing ponytail and had a small frame.

Celine Scott is our little group's fourth member. Celine is slightly taller than Angela and resembles Austin in that she is a bit more reserved. However, her dirty blond hair, which is always about shoulder length and which I love to watch shift and shimmer when she moves, and her gray blue eyes, which constantly seem to be dancing.

There are several reasons why our group of four is significant to us, but the primary one is probably that we never judge one another or try to date one another. Yes, we are all unmarried. Either have been forever, or have been for a while. We can all really unwind and be ourselves when we are all together. We've all witnessed each other in happy and sad moments, but mostly in good ones. We've all seen each other ill, buzzed, or intoxicated, but we never fail to assist each other when we need it.

James was setting up a new router in his computer system while in his guest room/office combo. Leaning out to grasp a dropped data line, he had his ear near his phone. Of course, it immediately decided to ring in his left ear. Before picking the phone and answering, he sprang back and held his ear while yelling some coarse words. "What?"

Okay, perhaps I'll just call again at a later time or on an other day.

"I'm sorry, Angela. I'll explain later, I guess. Why is that?"

"Just wanted to let you know that I could be running a little behind tonight. fifteen minutes, roughly."

"Oh, right,"

Just hold off on saying or doing anything significant until I arrive.

"True, there are a lot of essential things happening in our lives. Okay, no issue there. Do you feel alright?"

I simply need to stop by the courthouse and pay a fine, so I'm good.

"Oops."

"A twenty five in a thirty five, indeed. I'll see you tonight, love." She was his favorite of the two women in their small group, he reflected as he hung up the phone. Of then, he had the same sentiments about Celine only last week. He could comprehend the continued practice of bigamy.

James prepared a bowl of bacon-wrapped sausages and tossed them in a light barbecue sauce for the forthcoming event. He then put some diet Cokes and a case of Miller Lites in the refrigerator and declared it good. The others would bring more food so they wouldn't go hungry while they wasted their Saturday night sitting around.

Around 5:30, he unlocked his front door, and shortly after Austin entered, he yelled, "Bring out the naked women!"

He yelled from the kitchen, "I'm afraid it's the wrong night and the wrong house." "You better be telling me everything if you know where we should be."

When he saw James setting the paper plates and glasses out, he remarked, "I was only daydreaming. You must admit that it is a wise idea."

"Top shelf, actually."

Need assistance?

"No, I'm almost ready. This group requires very little upkeep."

Regardless of whose house we use, I think it's amazing how we all just make ourselves at home.

In fact, we might all live in the same one.

I wouldn't go nearly that far, I believe.

"Angela, by the way, will be a few minutes late."

Celine entered the room shortly after and said, "Oh, how I detest winter. It is quite depressing."

The season's blues, Austin said.

Whatever you choose to name it, it's still miserable and appears to last forever.

At least snow isn't falling,

Right now, I'd welcome snow only for a change of scenery.

"Are you going to be grumpy tonight?"

"Obviously not. In fact, just whining about it makes me feel better. Hey, Angela, where are you? She always arrives before me."

She had to stop and pay a fee before she could go home and change, James informed her.

"Fine? What is fine for?"

CHAPTER 2

"Let her tell you the tale," I said.

Oh, did you get your new comforter, curtains, and other things?

"I did, take a look at it, and let me know what you think."

She returned a little later and informed him, "Nice. You actually performed well; it's just unfortunate that it's so masculine."

You mean you haven't noticed that I'm a man?

"Of sure, but I just expected you to be a little more impartial, you know? Kind of in the middle."

"Sorry. I suppose it implies you can no longer join me in bed."

As if that were ever going to happen.

Hey, you nearly did it the evening of Gil and Wendy's wedding celebration.

"I was definitely wasted that evening. How you brought me home is still a mystery to me."

I don't recall anything about any of that, so neither do I.

After a while, Angela showed in and declared, "I need a cool beer to drown my sorrows." James gave her a chilled drink as she joined the group and patiently waited for her to take a sizable sip.

"In case you were wondering, the cost of a standard speeding ticket is $120. More if your ticket is for driving more than 10 miles over the speed limit that is posted. For the next month, I won't be eating out or doing anything else."

The four of them finished their meals, moved to the living room, and settled into chairs with end tables for their beverages. Before he replied, Austin turned to glance around and grinned "It appears that we are all enraged with one another. On this love seat, Celine and I are positioned similarly to how you and Angela are on the opposite ends of the couch." While they were eating, they conversed; Celine and Angela discussed getting stopped by attractive police, while Austin and James stayed out of the conversation. Angela recounted where and how she obtained her ticket.

They returned to the living room after James placed a bowl of salty nibbles on the coffee table and ordered beers for everyone after their plates were empty. They discussed their lives since their last meeting a few weeks ago for the next 30 to 45 minutes or so, but then James stated, "I have a thought. Something to divert our attention from work, the miserable weather, or whatever."

What is that, Angela enquired.

"Each of us chooses a period in our past that, for whatever reason, was significant to us or served as a turning point in our lives. Share that with the rest of us after that."

Any moment in our lives, Austin questioned?

"Yes, when I was a child, adolescent, or whatever. It may be humorous, sad, obscene, or frightening."

I'd have to consider that one, damn.

Angela concurred, "And I would." "So James, how are you doing? Do you have a plan for your story considering that this is your idea?"

"Sure, I do. I suppose there are a few, but only one immediately comes to me."

I'll grab more beers, Austin exclaimed, leaping to his feet.

Celine continued, "Okay, let's sit in a circle on the floor for James's story. James, are you going to try to make Angela and I look bad by telling this story?"

"Nope, but that's all I'm going to say up front," she replied. They sat in a small circle as soon as the coffee table was moved out of the way, and James continued, "Before I begin, I just have one thing to say. None of us has the authority to evaluate the storyteller. If one of us does something, well, you all probably understand what I mean by now. After all, we're going to be discussing the past."

Angela responded while grinning, "You've made your point, but now tell us a story. in depth."

"We'll keep an eye on the specifics. I simply want to express how much what happened amazed me on many levels. Because of this event, at least in some aspects, I felt like I suddenly matured. It truly had a significant impact on me. Okay, so this was back when I was twenty-one years old. I was still residing at home while completing some makeup credits in order to earn my BA. I asked my buddy Peyton Brooks out to supper after we had run into each other. Actually, beer and hamburgers. In any case, she agreed. I rang her doorbell and that's when the whole moment that will live in my mind began."

Oh hello James, come in, said Kelly Brooks.

"Hello, Mrs. Brooks I was planning on taking Peyton out for a burger and a beverage. Is she ready?"

Are you certain it was for this evening?

Yes, I had seen her earlier today at the mall.

"Oh no."

"Why, is there a problem?"

"She's not here, James. Peyton invited a man named Brad over, and the two of them left after Peyton informed him that she wouldn't be returning until very late."

"Oh."

"James, I'm really sorry. Even though I know this is awkward, all I can do is apologize."

Mrs. Brooks, Peyton is 21 years old; it is her responsibility to apologize, not yours.

I'm not sure why, but could I get you something to drink, perhaps a Coke?

Yes, thank you.

At that point, James turned to face the others and remarked, "I was at a loss for what to think or do at the time. Peyton had disappointed and humiliated her, so I felt bad for her.

CHAPTER 3

Austin asked, grinning, "What did this Mrs. Brooks look like James?" as he turned to face him.

"really quite similar to Peyton. Medium-length dark hair that is practically brown in color makes her really gorgeous in a more mature sense. Actually, I believed she was more attractive than her daughter in certain ways."

And what age was she?

She could have been older or younger, but at that moment I could only surmise that she was in her late forties. James finished some of his beer before continuing.

"James, will you please call me Kelly?"

Thank you; I will.

"I'm sorry to report, James, but this is not the first time she has pulled this ruse. We both know that even if she isn't yet aware of it, the way I didn't raise her to treat people will come back to bite her."

I won't stay because I don't want to ruin your evening, Kelly.

"I'm fine, and it's nice to see you again. Don't worry. What else have you been doing except attending college?"

That's all, then go to work helping Dad with his plumbing.

"I just realized you had to be twenty-one now,"

"I am. in reality, three extra months."

"Do you want anything added to your Coke, James? To give you a taste of J.D."

"That would be good, I agree. Wait, I have a better suggestion. You and I can go find that burger and a beverage or something if you grab your purse."

"Well let's get this straight, I don't view spending the evening with you as a waste at all. Are you sure you want to squander your evening with me?"

I accept your offer and thank you, Kelly remarked after grinning and examining the young man standing next to her.

Before James could continue, Angela did the same and questioned him, "Is this going where I think it's going?" James shifted back till he could lean back on the couch.

All you have to do is wait to witness love.

Is this a lengthy tale?

Just wait and see, I suppose. He proceeded to recount his story as she stuck her tongue out at him, reclined on the couch next to him, and silently sipped her beer.

I even wrapped her arm in mine as we were leaving and asked her, "Where would you like to go?" She responded, "I'd like to go to Connelly's."

When I quickly glanced at her, she grinned and said, "Relax James, I'm buying."

That wouldn't be proper, I say.

It would be ideal, and once we get there, I'll explain why it will be ideal to you.

For how we're dressed, isn't that location a touch posh?

We're alright, but if sitting in the bar area will help you feel better, we'll do that.

"That would make me feel more at ease." She made a tiny turn in her seat to observe me drive.

"James, I fail to comprehend why Peyton would do such a blunder. You're a really decent man who is also pretty attractive and endearing."

"Many thanks, Kelly. I must say that, looking back, I'm not really sorry she left me."

"Now that I know, you're just being brave,"

"Definitely not."

In the bar, we located a corner table, and when the server verified my identification, we were soon enjoying our first drinks while perusing the menu. I chose the osso bucco, while Kelly had the scallops and vegetables with a salad. I grinned and asked Kelly, "Okay, so explain how this is amazing," as soon as the waitress had left.

"Really, it's fairly easy. You know, her father gives me money to pay for her education bills, and she is free to spend whatever extra money that is left over. I believe that she should cover the cost of our evening."

She won't be happy about that, I'm certain of it.

"It's really ideal because of it. I will explain everything to her father if she complains to him, and he won't be happy with her either."

So your ex-husband and you still get along well?

"We've become more tolerant and civil, and we even agree on how to care for and treat Peyton. It appears that we made a few errors there."

"You gave it your all. Even with wonderful parenting, kids don't always respond positively."

"For someone who has never raised children, that seems pretty intelligent."

"I just watch and try to learn from it," she said.

Kelly responded with a smile, "Let's test your ability to observe. Describe our waitress for me."

She is attractive, and her short skirt is supposed to draw attention.

So you were aware of her.

"I did, of course—I'm young and unmarried. However, I'm already focusing on an attractive woman who unquestionably deserves it."

Oh James, you are just too smooth, please accept my gratitude. Before dinner arrived, we completed the first drink and began the second. We spoke while eating and eventually had a third drink.

To Peyton for paying for this great evening and for organizing for us to spend this time together, I raised my glass and said.

Yes, that is how much we owe her. I'll sure you've been curious about my age, she said after pausing to smile. She paused once more and said, "You do, as evidenced by your smile, but you're too much of a gentlemen to ask, so I'll just tell you. I'm 41 years old."

"And you should be aware that you don't appear it. You don't appear to be Peyton's mother's age. If you had told me that you became pregnant at the age of 15, I wouldn't have questioned it."

Oh James, we do need to extend this evening.

"Hope we succeed. Should we return to your home while I can still transport us there without incident?"

Yes, that could be a smart move.

Angela stated: "James, hold on, I want to switch to water or anything else instead of this beer. To hear the rest of this narrative, I want to be completely awake."

Angela and Celine both stood up, and Celine remarked, "I agree, Angela. We won't want to miss this, in my opinion."

Angela turned to face James as she halted midway to the kitchen.

Of course, it all depends on how specific he is in his account.

"There is that, after all, he is a male."

Angela sat down next to James on the floor once more when the women returned, but this time she turned and laid on her back, placing her head on his leg. Celine continued to sit on the floor and leant back against the side chair. James questioned her, "To what do I owe this honor?"

As you continue to relate this story, I want to see your face.

If you believe you can rattle me, think again.

"Oh, honey, I don't want to frighten you. I don't want to miss anything, in fact. Please go ahead."

"Good, then." I followed Kelly inside after we returned to her house in safety.

If you'll pardon me, James, I'd want to change out of these clothes and get comfy for a moment.

Of course Kelly, go at your own pace.

As she made her way up the stairs, she remarked, "There's some scotch in the little bar.

Thank you, but I believe I've met my quota for the evening. I went to the visitor restroom, took care of business, washed my hands, and took a quick look in the mirror. I went back to the living room and sat down on the sofa because my hair was, for the most part, still alright and my shirt was tucked in.

I heard her come down the open stairs approximately five minutes later. I stood up and moved till I could see her, at which point I simply grinned and watched her tumble down. When she approached me, I didn't try to avoid staring at her. I said, "You look wonderful. She was dressed in a light, short silk cover that was worn over a silk lounge attire. Not so short as to be overt or sleazy, but what I could see of her legs—and there was a lot—I really enjoyed. Very good, Kelly, and you certainly appear at ease. "James, I'm pleased you like it. I hope you don't mind, but this will allow me to skip dressing later and just slip into bed."

CHAPTER 4

"Now Kelly, I'm your loyal slave."

She gave me a cheek kiss and remarked, "I believe Peyton is crazy for standing you up, as I previously stated. Join me in the chair."

We sat close to one another on that big sofa, and I truly was her willing servant. After that, I don't really recall much of what we discussed. I recall doing my best to look her in the eye, and I believe I succeeded, but I also caught a few glances at her legs. We gradually leaned back until she had her feet tucked up under her butt and I had my stocking feet extended out beneath the coffee table. I could see a lot more of her legs as she gently turned to face me and opened up her robe a bit at the bottom."

"How come I've never heard this story before?" Austin interrupted James.

"I suppose it's one of those things that simply never came up. Even though I'll never forget it, I've filed it away in my memory throughout the years."

You can see most of her legs up now, at least.

I did, indeed. Celine questioned, "So okay, what happened next stud?" as James's hand and arm were draping over Angela's midriff as she continued to observe him. James didn't even notice it.

At that point, I wish I could recall every small detail. I recall that we spoke a little longer, and that my hand eventually landed on her leg halfway up from her knee. Right around that time, I gave her my first kiss, and she eagerly reciprocated it.

Kelly and I exchanged kisses, and as we did so, she said, "I knew I'd like the way you kiss James. I drew her closer to me without saying anything, and then we had a much longer and deeper kiss. Oh my God, James, you are so perilous.
"I'm not even close to being as dangerous as you are. Kelly, you are incredibly attractive and seductive." We started kissing again, and as we kissed, my hands began to explore as I gradually rolled onto my back with her on top of me. My hands could no longer feel anything but her warm butt and a thin flutter of underpants because her slippery silk robe had moved up. One of my hands slid up under her robe and, it turned out, under her top until I was examining the area that, of course, should have had some sort of bra."
That's all the information I'll go into, James replied as he bowed his head to Angela.
Austin pleaded, "No wait, don't stop there, damn."
Celine remained silent while paying close attention to James.
I'm not sure if I want you to stop or keep going, Angela finally murmured.
Celine and you may decide, but I believe halting would be beneficial.

"But what took place? I don't know, eventually or whatever " We naturally made love. I had sex with an elderly woman."

"And?"

"And it was wonderful. No, that was fantastic. Tell us more about the feelings without mentioning the act itself, if that makes sense.

"We spent a considerable amount of time in her bed since she was attentive and passionate. She was about twice as old as I was throughout that time, but I didn't realize it.

Says Kelly "Lordy, James Wish we could stay in bed together all night." Then she shouted, "Peyton's home," and we heard the downstairs front door open.

I exclaimed, "Oh sh*t, now what?"

Now we simply remain where we are.

"She won't enter this room?"

"No. When she notices that I am not moving and assumes that I am asleep, she will pass past the door, perhaps pause, and then continue to her room." As Peyton ascended the stairs, Kelly drew the sheet up over us, got even closer to me, and laid her head on my arm. For a brief while, even though I couldn't see Peyton, I could feel her presence, and then Kelly remarked, "She's gone to her room now."

"Perhaps I should leave here,"

"Don't leave yet, James. When will I next see you."

Would you be willing to?

"It would suit me just well. James I should know by now that what we're doing won't work, but at the very least, I'd like to see you again. Kelly, you are such an outstanding and beautiful woman, I can't believe that you're still single. I'd like to see you and make love to you at least once more.

"I get to decide. I simply didn't want to engage in all of that again after the divorce. Now have a peek at me. You're in my bed, and I can't stop wanting more of you."

It can be a sentinel moment in your life.

"Only time will tell, but it very well may be. James, may I give you a call in a few days?"

"Sure," you say. We continued to spend some time together, but I was unable to spend the night. We shared another passionate kiss as she led me to the door before I got dressed and departed. The following time I saw my friend Deke, I told him about the older woman and how hot I thought she was, among other things. I confessed to him that it was difficult for me to accept that I had mistreated an elderly woman. He attempted to be smart as he said to me, "Man, you've got to learn to be more picky. more like myself." I laughed at that one and informed him that, in his opinion of being picky, a lady should have the majority of her teeth and take a bath at least once every week—at least during the summer.

Then James asked Angela, "Well, did I startle you?" as he cast a downward glance at her.

CHAPTER 5

"I must admit that you surprised me. She wasn't married, which is a plus."

No, we were both pretty law abiding.

Didn't it feel strange to be in bed with her while her daughter was right down the hall, Celine questioned?

"It felt incredibly strange, but not to the point where I wanted to flee."

"I assume you were back with her then."

Ten days later, it was wonderful once more, but it was the last time.

Angela said him, "So that event truly touched you," while his hand was still on her stomach. She then placed her hand on his.

"Really, it did. But I doubt I'll ever be able to explain why. Like, if she had been my age, I would have continued using terminology from my time in college. Slang or some of the "in" words, perhaps with an attempt to appear cool. It's like I behaved older because being around her made me feel older. Instead of feeling like a rambunctious schoolboy, I appreciated feeling more like a grown man. She made me feel both worldly and like a student because I had learnt so much from her. instance: patience. I give up because I have no idea where to start."

"Oh, I believe I comprehend completely. Have you ever considered that you truly did rock her world? She felt young, appealing, and vibrant because of things like you, among other factors, I'm sure. Instead of being a resentful divorcee, you reminded her what it was like to be a woman still in her prime. You two were compatible, in my opinion."

"Could be. I certainly hope so."

Have you seen her since then, Austin questioned?

"No. Of course, I've given her a lot of thought over the years, but I've never returned. Most likely, she doesn't even reside there anymore."

What's up with Peyton?

"I don't know what to do. I definitely didn't feel anything for her. I was merely unconcerned."

After finishing their last round of beer and talking about relationships in general, Celine embraced James and thanked him for being such a sensitive stud.

I adore you, you're welcome.

Austin then added, "Personally, I would have preferred to hear at least a little bit more information. Consequently, you two did meet later. How went that?"

"Really not much different from the first time, except that Peyton was never even mentioned. However, I found out that she had moved into her own apartment a few months later." He then asked, "Well, do any of you have a tale to share or do you need more time?" after turning to face Celine and Angela.

I've got a quick one," Angela remarked.

"Great, let's settle back in."

Celine sat next to James this time, but on the couch rather than the floor, and Angela sat across from James and closer to Austin. "Okay," Angela continued, "I was seventeen years old when this occurred. It's nothing like James's, but it has always been a beautiful memory tucked away in my memories of those trying adolescent years. Mom and Dad were going through a difficult time, and we were living on the south side of the city. Despite appearing to be on the verge of separation, they persisted. As you might guess, that caused a lot of chaos in my environment, and to make matters worse, my boyfriend Roger began acting strangely. Then I learned that he was seeing Junior Kendrick via a friend. We did know each other, even though she wasn't precisely a buddy. Roger and I ended up breaking up because of our dispute, which was predictable. Now since Roger was such a jerk, I also had to deal with the parent issue. My life at the moment seemed truly miserable.

To my astonishment, Mom and Dad told me I was old enough to stay home alone after deciding they wanted to go for a few days to work on their problems. Naturally, they provided a brief list of items that were prohibited. You know, no drinking or smoking, no parties, etc. I had intended on lounging in the backyard and avoiding trouble because I didn't need them to be angry with me at all. In any case, I wasn't in the mood for more."

The Carlson family resided next door to us. They had two children: Annie, who was away at college, and Drew, who was around my age. He always seemed kind enough, but for some reason I never felt his name matched him and I didn't particularly enjoy it. We would bump into one another and converse. But for some reason, we were never particularly attracted to one another. That all changed on the Saturday when Mom and Dad left for their hideout. I was seated on the back porch around midday when Drew shouted to me from his driveway.

Hey Angela, how are things?

"Dear Drew: Oh, it's quiet, not much is happening. What's up, dude?"

"Oh, I guess it's about the same. On weekends, Mom and Dad are likely doing whatever the hell they do."

"They go everywhere, don't they?"

"Yeah."

"Got time for something, or a Coke?"

Sure, I have the entire day. I brought him a drink, and we chatted outside in the shade of our tiny back porch.

Drew, don't you two — what's his name — Gary — frequently get together?

He started a job last week, therefore this weekend he is working.

"How is working with your dad going?"

"Okay, I suppose. I make a little money, but it's not a big issue. Simply lounging around this weekend?"

I have severe instructions to behave myself because my parents are away—you know, the list of restrictions.

CHAPTER 6

"I recognize what you mean, yes. Hello, I was aware of your boyfriend. I'm sorry things went south for you."

I can't believe he did that, so thank you.

"And Junior Kendrick, of course. Why in the world did he think that? He had you as his girlfriend, after all. Not even in your class, Junior."

"What a relief, Drew. I've been feeling fairly unattractive and uninteresting lately, so it was good."

"Well, I don't need any special abilities to recognize your attractiveness. Want to spend the day hanging out together?"

"Sure, if you'd like to join me, I was just going to lay out in the sun for a little."

I'll go change. "Cool, I'd like that."

Welcome back, please."

Angela turned around and uttered, "You know, Drew seemed like a typical guy. I'm not sure what I was expecting, but he was alright. I guess he had a very good body, but as I reflect, I believe it was the way he conducted himself. He appeared to be just being himself. You see, he wasn't trying to impress me or pretend to be someone he wasn't; I just felt at ease around him. Like, perhaps after all, we could be great pals.

Celine enquired, "How did he look you in the eye? I think that's important."

"He was fairly skilled at it. He simply glanced there a few times because I was already quite developed and was wearing a simple pullover with a neckline that showed plenty."

"I appreciate the direction this is taking."

James smiled and said, "So do I.

"He returned home in his bathing suit, and we went outside to the backyard where I had spread an old blanket on the grass. Oh, and I was now wearing a bikini. My tacky lime green and pink one, I believe, was the one that wasn't too showing.

"Angela I'll mention this right now and probably again shortly. You appear to be attractive. I imply extremely heated. Roger has to be really insane."

"Regards, Drew. Thanks to that guy, I certainly don't feel all that special right now."

Okay, let's discuss topics that are more upbeat than ex-boyfriends.

Drew, who are you seeing right now?

"Nobody unique. Sort of like running into someone I know and then doing stuff together. I'm already routinely broke right now. Dad gave me a loan, and of course I had to pay it back. That was one of my foolish decisions. likely one of many."

"That makes it seem like you don't really like who you are." I warned him, "You're not going to tan very well in that posture," as he turned on his side to face me.

I must also sun on my side to avoid turning into an Oreo cookie. I hadn't laughed so hard in a while till then. I'm certain that I laughed more loudly than the joke merited looking back. Have you ever had the impression that your life is in a rut, Angela?

"Yes, I suppose, occasionally. I know I have college in the near future, so that will occupy my attention for a while."

"You leaving for school?"

"I'm afraid I'll have to study at home instead. You?"

"Nope. student who stays at home, like you. Having no extra money."

We chatted while lying there, shifting positions occasionally to get the ideal all-over tan. He backed up a bit and said, "Damn you have a cute shape, Angela," as I lay on my stomach. I gave him a thank-you smile and turned to face him as I rested there. Would you like another Coke or something? He enquired. I have a few here at home.

Yes, but take them from our refrigerator. A minute later, he returned and crouched down near me.

I sort of screamed and quickly turned on my side when he placed one of those ice-cold Coke cans on my back. He had the cutest, most evil smile I'd ever seen as he gazed down at me. "Damn you Drew." I tried to act like I was mad but what did I do? I smiled at him. "You'll pay for that one," and I quickly poured some of my icy drink on him before he could retreat. He said something I don't remember and rolled out of my reach but I shook my can and sprayed him. Of course he did the same and a minute later we were both covered in sticky soda and our cans were empty, but we were laughing and having a blast together.

I looked down at myself and said, "Drew we better rinse off before this turns sticky and before we can even go inside." He saw the hose and without a word he turned it on and gently bathed me. God my head was swimming with conflicting feelings. We really didn't know each other all that well and here I was allowing his hand to touch me all over as he rinsed me off. He had a...his boxer style suit had a tent and... I finally stopped him and said, "We...we better go in and towel down or something."

We didn't make it. He dropped the hose and our arms went around each other and we fell into a kiss that I can still remember."

Celine was motionless as she waited for Angela to say more but she had stopped. "Damn Angela, don't stop there, what happened?"

"We almost made love right there on the blanket. I mean right there in my backyard where we could be seen. I don't remember now how we managed to keep from going farther, but we did stop. It's a good thing too because I wasn't on the pill or anything and of course he wasn't prepared either. We really did get into each other and he didn't go home until almost midnight. We'd talk or watch a movie or whatever and then end up in each other's arms again, but by about ten or so both of us had settled down some. We spent all of Sunday together and I even cooked for him." Angela smiled and her eyes looked like she was far away as she added, "I made some terrible meals, but we both ate what I fixed and he never complained."

"Is he still in the area?"

"No. We were together a few times after that, but he got a chance to go to Ohio State and then we moved so I don't have any idea where he is today. But I'll bet he's married and has three kids by now."

"So what about you Austin? Got a story to share with us," Angela asked.

"As a matter of fact I do have, but let's save it until the next time. I'd like to tell it before I've had three beers."

"And you Celine?"

"Same answer, next time."

The Friday after their gathering, Celine called James and told him, "I just wanted to thank you for sharing your sweet story. I thought about that a lot afterward, and it isn't hard to understand why it had such an impact on you."

"You know, at the time, it really was mostly about the sex for me. I mean at that moment anyway. But...afterward it was so much more, especially as time passed and I looked back at it from a more mature perspective."

"I'm sure. You do realize don't you that Kelly, your Mrs. Robinson, seduced you."

CHAPTER 7

"Of course. As the evening progressed it was in my mind to seduce her, but I was an amateur and moved far too slow."

"I think that just added to the experience that Kelly was hoping for. Intentional or not, you handled yourself great. You both brought something to the evening that the other wanted and needed. I have no doubt that you changed her life that night."

"I just hope she didn't have regrets afterward."

Celine laughed and said, "Her only regret would have been because she stopped seeing you after the second time."

"I'm glad you and Angela weren't disappointed in me, or at least I hope you weren't."

"Are you kidding? I loved your story and just watching Angela looking up at you, I could tell that she felt the same way."

"I feel better knowing that. What do you suppose Austin will tell us the next time?"

"I can't imagine, but don't be surprised if he is a little more graphic if it involves sex."

"I certainly don't mind, so it will be up to you and Angela to keep him under control."

Celine laughed told him, "I'm not too worried. Have you heard from him?"

"Yeah, he called and wanted to hear more of the juicy details."

"I figured he would, did you share them with him?"

"Yeah, or at least a few of them. You know, how she looked and how it felt to touch her and respond to me."

"Poor Austin, I'll bet he was drooling. How did she look by the way?"

"Celine, you didn't want to hear any of that. Have you been hiding just a touch of pervert from the rest of us?"

There was a light lilt to her voice as she smiled into the phone.

"No, of course not, I mean was she wrinkled?"

"Not at all, she wasn't that old, just older than me by twenty years. Her skin was smooth and soft and fair, and she liked to have me...sorry, I'm getting carried away."

"Now you're teasing me."

"Just trying to behave myself love."

"No you're not, you're teasing me. Baiting me in to asking you for more details and more questions."

"You don't want to hear the details about our coupling I'm sure."

"Of course not, but as I listened to you tell your story last Saturday night, I could almost feel the sexual tension in the room when she came down the stairs."

"I still can, and like I said, she moved fast enough that I didn't have time to worry about what I should or shouldn't do. It was all so intense and fast and... over far too soon."

"James, I'm seeing a part of you that I've never seen before. I think your story was so sweet and so...so significant. And like you said, on so many levels. You two were so good for each other. I'm happy for you that you have those memories."

"Thanks Celine. I can't wait to hear your story...or stories."

"They will be tame compared to yours, so don't expect a lot. It's so hard for me to share memories and convey the same impact that the situation had on me at the time."

"I know exactly what you mean."

"What did you think of Angela's story?"

"She was at a very unstable part of her life right then and Drew came to her at just the right time. She needed him, or someone like him so much right then. I'm surprised that they lost contact so soon."

"I am too, but you know...the emotions of a teenaged girl and all."

"I don't know, but I'm sure it was an important time for her. I'll bet she did look hot that day in her ugly bikini."

"I'm sure she did, especially to Drew." Then she changed the subject and asked, "James, were you aware that you were caressing Angela's belly?"

"I was what?"

"When you were telling your story and she had her head on your leg. Your hand was across her belly."

"Oh, yeah I remember that, but I wasn't caressing her. She would have slapped me I'm sure."

"I don't mean you were putting moves on her. More like in your mind you were seeing Kelly and as you talked your hand would move over Angela's belly or your thumb would slowly move back and forth."

"Guess I didn't realize. Did Angela say something to you later?"

"Not a word, so I guess it was no big deal. I was just curious."

James's reminiscing about Kelly had put her in his thoughts again. He thought about what he had told the others and hoped he was able to convey the significance of that time in his life. He also found himself driving past her house late that Saturday afternoon.

He saw her when he was still two houses from her. She was bending over a small bush and nipping at it with little shears. She was in brown shorts and his eyes went straight to her sweet butt and legs. He slowly drove past her and told himself not to stop. He told himself that again as he was turning around at the corner. She was still there when he pulled up to the curb in front of her house. She didn't look up until she heard him close his car door. She straightened up and looked for a second before she dropped her nippers and almost ran to him as he walked toward her. Their arms went around each other as she said, "James, I can't believe it's you."

"It's me and I have to say, you look as fantastic as before; just as I remember you."

CHAPTER 8

"Oh my god, my hair is a mess and I'm grubby from working in the yard."

"You look great Kelly, it's good to see you again."

"Please come in and...please stay long enough so we can talk."

"I'd like that if you have time."

"I do." She took his hand in hers and she led the way around the house to the backdoor saying, "I'm too dirty to go in the front so I hope you'll forgive me."

"Of course, It's you I came to see. You've been in my thoughts a lot lately."

She stopped and turned to look at him as she smiled. "Have you really thought about me?"

"Of course, many, many times, but more so lately for some reason."

"I think of us quite often too, James." She led him in through the mud room and to the kitchen saying, "Go on in and I'll go wash up. Can I get you anything first?"

"No, I'm fine until you join me." As he waited in the living room, he looked around and smiled. She had a new sofa, but it was in the same place, and the open staircase was just the same. He didn't even sit down right away. He just smiled inside as he quickly relived their first tryst. That time when he was so consumed by her charm and beauty and allure.

When she came down the stairs this time she was wearing short red shorts and a modest halter top. He smiled at her and as she neared him he said, "I have to say again, I don't know how you do it, but you look as good as you did the last time I saw you."

She put her arms around him and told him, "I'm so glad you stopped James."

"I drove by once telling myself not to stop, but as you can see that didn't work."

"Why wouldn't you stop?"

"I wasn't sure how...I don't know I guess. Fear maybe. Fear that you wouldn't want to see me again."

Of course I want to see you again."

Kelly, I still remember you coming down those stairs in that red filmy outfit of yours and I remember how I was overwhelmed by you."

She led him to the sofa and sat down pulling him down next to her. She was sitting on the edge of the cushion and half turned toward him as she held his hand and asked him, "How have you been? Are you married?"

"I've been fine and I'm not married." He made a point of looking at her left hand and added, "And I see that you aren't either."

"Almost, but we both pulled back. I still see him...or rather we still see each other. Now how is it that you're still single?"

"Like you, almost one time, but it wasn't right. She went her way and I went mine."

Before asking him, "Not even a significant other?" she leaned in and gave him a quick, gentle kiss.

"No." Peyton was never addressed during their conversation. Then James revealed to her, "I have three pals who are very close to me, and we get together once every two weeks." Then he revealed to her what he had told them about their time spent together.

Kelly responded as she gave him a concerned look, "What did they say, oh my god? Those guys had names for me, I bet."
two women and one more man. They praised my narrative and expressed happiness that I could have such wonderful recollections. They claimed that we had been beneficial to one another. That moment, you and I needed one another."

"They were obviously correct, and I believe I like your pals. Maybe the need was more of a want than a need. I knew I wanted us to make love when we went out to lunch that Friday night. Although I thought it was absurd and didn't think it would happen, I still desired it. I kept telling myself that I was too old to be thinking those things, but it didn't work."

"You were not too old to have those thoughts or aspirations, and I wanted you too, Kelly. You are still not close to being too old for that."

"I'm grateful. How did you inform them? How much did you tell them, specifically?"

"I gushed to them about how stunning you were and are. As I gazed at your legs and eagerly became your slave, I informed them about you going down the stairs. I told them about our kissing, our flirting, and how we made love in your bed before making love once more. I assured them that I would always remember our interactions." He told her his narrative while their eyes were fixed on each other, and thereafter he questioned her, "Did you make the right choice when you said no more after the second time?"

"I'm not certain. No, it was obviously the proper choice, but I really wanted to keep seeing you. I should never have flirted with you in the first place; that was my mistake. When Peyton abandoned you, I should not have allowed you in, but I did because I felt bad for you. It was so unnecessary and had to hurt so badly."

"I owe you for the fact that I don't recall hurting. You saved me, and I'm still happy that she left that night with the other person." He gave her another kiss as he came in close to her and added, "It seems as though there was no time between when I last visited and now. I still enjoy kissing you despite how wonderful you look."

"You're older and perhaps more attractive," she said. The insignificant kisses and touches were occurring more frequently. They injured one other because they desired each other so badly, but they were attempting to restrain themselves. Are you certain that you don't want something, James?

"There you are, Kelly, and I need you. Please don't say no to me. I long to sense our reunion."

Because she knew she had to have him once more, Kelly's heart was thumping. Her fight was over the moment he declared his desire for her. James, I want you too. He undressed her and left her clothing all over the couch and floor when they got up. He followed closely after her as he watched her move her bare ass in front of him as she led him to the stairs. He stopped her on the steps, put his hands on her hips, knelt, and began kissing her behind. Oh my God James," she said before continuing to climb. He turned her around and pulled her towards him at the top of the stairs as his hands briefly probed her. His first encounter with her left him feeling so overwhelmed that he mostly followed her lead. But this time, he was impatient since he was aware of what was going to happen.

Kelly, I want you so much, damn it. They eventually found her bedroom, where they had their first kiss and he undressed. They were able to explore, kiss, and use their hands this time. Following their passionate encounter, they took a nap before continuing their playful banter. She had tiny, delicate breasts, and a practically shaven mound, which he loved to feel with his hands.

CHAPTER 9

She exalted his freshness and vigor. His desire to win her favor and the gossamer-warm veil of flattery he draped over her. Kelly didn't have his endurance, but if she grew too worn out, all she needed to do was lie down and wait for him to find her. Even though it took them some time to get out of bed, it seemed like it only took a few moments. Kelly grinned and whispered, "Damn you. "We couldn't engage in romantic activity again, I reminded myself, but I couldn't help it. I believe I ought to meet your pals and let them know you were to blame for everything. because you're simply too alluring to resist."

"They wouldn't believe you because they knew me. To them, I'm just another guy."

"So they need assistance,"

"Would you be interested in meeting them? No, it would be difficult knowing that they are aware that we made out."

"So? We have all probably made love to someone. Look at the mother holding the infant. No one takes one look at her or her partner and says, "Wow, those two screwed for sure.""

But that's different.

"Okay, but if you want to meet them, we can go out to supper. Connelly may."

Very humorous.

"I'm for real,"

"I'll consider it. Even though I'd like to meet them, I'm not sure if I could handle it."

Will asking the others be helpful?

"Perhaps it would," They went downstairs, but instead of dressing, Kelly led him to the door, where they kissed again and he departed vowing to call her soon.

James called Angela on Sunday afternoon because he didn't want to wait. Following their story-telling, he had already wished to speak with her.

Hello, busy?

What are you doing? I was, but I'm not right now.

Well, I wanted to check to see whether you had changed your mind about me after hearing my story.

"Naturally, I don't despise you. Okay, let's meet for coffee at Kelly's."

He said, "On my way," put down his phone, and walked toward the eatery. He was standing there just in front of her and grinned as she approached him. After giving her a cheek kiss, he invited her inside where they got coffee and chatted.

Angela questioned him, "Why," adding, "Are you so worried that I'll think less of you for sleeping with this Kelly?"

I merely wanted to be certain.

Well, you can relax, right?

Is it true what Celine said about me touching your belly that night?

"Generally speaking, you were. You stopped when I put my hand on yours, but you would restart if I moved my hand."

"Oh. I'm sorry; it wasn't my intention."

Did Celine really say it wasn't okay?

"No...no, she just asked whether I knew I was doing that," I replied.

"In fact, it was rather pleasant. You were so engrossed in your story that you would occasionally look down at me and smile. The entire time was filled with compassion and absolute tranquility. I could almost feel what you were going through because of how well you conveyed your story. Well, we were experiencing what you had described. I couldn't have been more content or happy. Even though I didn't want the narrative to end when it did, unlike Austin, I also didn't want to hear all the juicy details "She then grinned at him.

"Angela...I passed Kelly's house yesterday," she said.

She answered with a smile, "Really, I'm not shocked. I'm talking about the memories you had just gone over again. Did it appear the same as you remembered?"

"very almost She was at the front of the car nibbling at a bush as I slowly drove by out of curiosity."

"And you stared at her as you slipped by her," Angela remarked while grinning once more.

"In fact, I was so shocked that she even resided there that I moved to the next street, turned around, and returned. I wouldn't give up. Although it was comforting to see her and learn that she was alright, I forced myself to continue."

James, you didn't quit, did you?

"Yes, I stopped," he replied as he turned back to her after taking a sip of his coffee. Angela didn't give him the sympathetic grin he was hoping for. She was out there tending to that bush in her shorts, as I stated, and she didn't even notice me.

She wouldn't have noticed if you had moved on, so you could have.

"Yeah."

Tell me the rest, James.

He disregarded their coffee and started the story. Except for one thing, he appeared to be a mature child repenting of his faults. He remained unconvinced. He misled his pal. He continued, "We exchanged a long embrace when she saw me, and she brought me inside."

"You didn't, James. Tell me that you didn't make out with her once more."

You initially believed the situation was amusing and understandable.

"You were a child at the time, naive. One of those things just happened, that's how it was. This time, it seemed like you were trying to find it, which isn't the same. By this time, she must be close to fifty."

CHAPTER 10

He was really taken off guard by her response. "I'm not certain that I can perceive many differences. Again, it was impromptu because I didn't anticipate seeing her. She is also forty-four."

"James, that is very different. Have you made out with her?"

"No." His falsehood was there. He didn't like himself very much at the time, primarily because he had lied to Angela. He was quick and a little forceful. No, but of course I thought of it.

As she spoke, she appeared to loosen up a bit "Of course you would think of that. How does it feel to see her again?"

"She hasn't really changed much. We had a lengthy conversation."

"And was embraced, what else? James, now be sincere."

"We shared a few kisses, and I suppose that's it. We talked, kissed, and exchanged hugs." He spoke quickly as he struggled to swallow the sour taste of his verbal transgression. I explained to her that there were four of us and that I had told you three about her.

So she is aware that we are now aware of your two making out?

"Yes."

"I'll bet she didn't think much of that," I said.

"Not initially, but we did discuss it. People make love all the time, Angela. regardless of age, marital status, or age range. You've had a romantic relationship. Life entails it."

"However, given the two of you are a very different ages, she might feel a little awkward. She must have been a little upset to learn that your pals get a glimpse into her private life."

James wasn't taking care of himself well. I requested that she meet you three, and she requested that she meet you three.

"I can't believe you, my god. You seemed like a more compassionate person to me."

Well, I told her that, so I'm asking you if the five of us could get together for dinner or something soon. He then shrugged his shoulders like a child and avoided making eye contact with her.

She added, "I'll accept a smile." "Austin, as we both know, would dearly love to meet her. And while I wouldn't mind meeting her, it would simply be a little weird. Hello Kelly, you're the elderly woman who enchanted James a few years ago."

"Just for the record, it was three years ago, and you're overreacting. You're overdramatizing everything."

"Not me. See if Celine shares your sentiments by asking her. But Austin would only be chanting your praises, so don't bother."

I'm sorry I let you down, Angela, but I just had to stop and see her when I saw her.

"And that's okay; I can see where you're coming from. That bothered me a little because you had me believing that you two had made out once more. I'll agree to meet her and all that, all right." She replied as she slightly leaned back, "Okay, I'll even admit that I'm interested in her. Let's go to Celine's house for dinner if she agrees."

Connelly's, that is.

She gave him another glance. "You had dinner with her there the night you made love for the first time."

Yes, it's a beautiful place.

"I've been there before, so I know. That's a nice touch, lover. Okay, Connelly's or wherever, but assuming Celine is on board, let's schedule it soon so we can...er, rather, so you can continue, is that clear?"

"That's fine with me. I appreciate your patience, and I'll be prepared to continue. Simply put, I want to stay in touch with her because I consider her a friend."

We both know that you do not see me as your friend in the same manner, Angela remarked with a smile.

True enough, he said while grinning.

Angela took his hand in hers as they exited the restaurant and apologized, "Sorry I got a little testy with you."

"That's fine; I'm sorry I frightened you. Regarding the fact that I made love to her, why would that have disturbed you?"

"I'm not sure. The initial experiences were...sweet and innocent in nature. You were practically a man, yet you were still rather innocent. I don't know, I guess I have no idea why, but it bothered me. When are you going to tell Austin what you did?"

"I'll probably give him a ring when I get home. Of course, I'll also inform him about the dinner. I'll also call Celine."

"When is the dinner on the weekend?"

"If that's okay with you."

"It will. Oh no, Austin and Celine's story will be told at that time."

"That's accurate. Okay, Friday evening."

She simply grinned and replied, "Perfect. Then, on Saturday night, we can discuss her."

He placed his hands on her shoulders as they approached her car and gave her a very light kiss on the lips before saying, "Thanks for listening to me and allowing me the chance to explain myself."

"Thank you so much. Just because I hold you in such high regard. You have the appropriate amount of bravado and are a cool guy. Not enough to prevent you from having empathy and compassion, but enough to let people know that you are a proud man of your gender. Then you pulled that prank on Kelly, and I was shaken. I assumed you were past all of that. We are a little more close than other buddies because we grew up together. We all think of each other a little differently than the ordinary friend because we are."

"Again, I apologize. For the record, you are my ideal friend. Maximum femininity mixed with a touch of feistiness, attractive, and compassionate."

CHAPTER 11

Before saying, "I should go before we get carried away with nice words," she grinned and expressed just a hint of surprise.

She watched as he turned away while waving and saying, "Hey...I liked having your head in my lap that night," as he moved a few steps toward his car. She was unsure of how to react to what he had just said.

While waiting at a stoplight, James used his cellphone to make a call to Celine. He greeted her and asked, "Hey, it's me, had a minute?" as the light turned green.

I have, hopefully, a lot of minutes left if I don't get killed by the moron in front of me.

Whereabouts are you?

About three miles from your location, on Greenfield.

Stop by if you have a moment because I have a question for you.

I won't be there for ten minutes, but I don't know where you are.

Immediately behind you, I'll be.

Celine followed James up the front walk as he left his car in the driveway. So James, what do you want to ask?

"Okay when we go inside? In reality, I have two inquiries for you."

"Okay."

She was asked, "Anything to drink?" by him.

No thanks. She remarked, "Okay, hit me with the first question," as they sat next to one another on the loveseat.

As with Angela, he lied about having sex with his 44-year-old friend when he told her about going to visit Kelly first. Tell me the rest, James.

You're not upset with me, then.

Keep going, it's not that far, so he did. "All right, so you two were on the...couch?

"Yeah."

And you held hands, conversed, kissed, and continued to converse.

"Yeah."

"James..."

"What?"

"You are experimenting with fire. Okay, I'll suppose you two didn't actually make love, but even if you did, you both have to have thought about it without a doubt."

"I certainly did, a lot. I merely wanted to know if you believed that I was acting erratically."

"You were, of course. That's OK, but I also get it. You yearned to see her again because talking about her enough triggered those recollections. You have the freedom to choose your own path because you're a big boy. Naturally, this does not guarantee that you will always make wise decisions. Although I already indicated that I understood, I'll add that I believe you should have left the past in the past."

Okay, how would you have responded if I had said that Kelly and I had made out?

I would have been more verbose about how poor your reasoning was and how you were meddling with Kelly's life, but otherwise, I assume, it was about the same.

"Kelly's?"

"No doubt. God, such a young woman It's pretty heavy to have a young boy make her over and want to make love to her. Say a male her age has already entered her life or will do so in the near future. He'll be compared to you by her. Is he as potent as you are? Does he possess your speed and endurance? She will still be aware that you approached her rather than the other way around, even if the answers to those questions were affirmative. She will have enticed a 24-year-old man into her bed."

"So that would be doing her a great disservice."

That's what I was thinking, but I'm not a 44-year-old with you in my bed.

"You have no idea how I'd be in bed," I said.

She remarked with a smirk, "Oh, so we'll start using foul language now? Remember when we made mud pies together? back behind the garage of your neighbors?"

"Yes, I recall it, and I recall that you frequently wore no top."

I must have been around eight years old.

"Yes, but even so...

I've moved past mud pies and am going topless, lothario.

"You still have your top on, I'll bet. It all relies on your surroundings and your companions."

"You have been impacted by Kelly, without a doubt. You need to know that Angela phoned me immediately after you left her at the restaurant to let me know that you would be calling and to explain why."

That's unfair; it's like playing two people off against one.

"Now don't look, but that is indeed it. We both believe your choice was not wise."

My preference is for Kelly to join the four of us for dinner at Conner's, as I assume she already told you.

"What? No, she didn't share that detail with me. Explain further."

"Well, Kelly is a friend, and all I want is for her to meet my best pals. Oh, and she is aware that you are all aware of our sexual encounters."

"This is becoming strange. And to think that it all began when you shared with us that adorable and somewhat innocent tale about you and Kelly." Okay, I'd like to meet this woman who makes you say and do silly things, she remarked, taking his hand in hers.

Okay, let's say Friday at Connelly's and start at 6:30.

"I'll attend. I wouldn't even mind missing this."

The response from Angela was "better than that," Celine, I appreciate your understanding. He kissed her cheek and said, "Thanks."

CHAPTER 12

I simply expressed my eagerness to meet her and possibly learn more about you two. I didn't say I understood. Celine turned to him at the entrance, grinned, gave him a soft kiss, and said, "I'm OK, James. I may be confused, but I still care about you. Oh, and if you're smart, you won't bring up the fact that I was topless while we were out by the old man's garage."

However, it was a terrific time.

Yes, it was, but just like with Kelly, the past cannot be changed.

"Oh, it was simply too clever. I'll see you on Friday night, "Celine then left him there in the doorway.

He last spoke to Austin. Once that was resolved, he could unwind and forget about everything—at least until Friday night. On the second ring, Austin caught it. Hey James, what's going on?

Are you arranging anything for Friday night?

What's going on, not till I visit my sister.

"Kelly is joining us for dinner."

"But wait, who are we?"

Celine and Angela

With Kelly, did you say?

"At Connelly's, of course."

"My sister can wait until Sunday while I'm there. What's the background of this change?" He shared the same facts with the two women when he shared his experience with them again. "She wasn't taken to bed by you? Why not, are you getting old?"

"She didn't put herself on hold until I showed up again, after all. She won't go to bed if I just walk in."

It's too bad.

You believe that I could have had another sexual encounter with her?

"Absolutely, why not? You both are aware that you are consenting adults. It's not like you needed approval from Miss Manners, the Pope, or whomever else."

"I suppose you're correct. Okay, Connelly's at 7:30 on a Friday night."

"All right, see you then." James simply shook his head and hung up. He had spoken with Angela, Celine, and Austin, and had gotten three different perspectives on how he ought to have behaved. It was expected that Austin would be the lone supporter of what he had truly done to Kelly.

He came to the conclusion that Celine and Angela's opinions were more significant to him as the evening went on since he felt that he shouldn't have put Kelly to bed. He grinned as he made that decision as he thought back on what it had been like to be with her once more. In addition, he realized that he needed to improve his personal life. His diagnosis was that he was vulnerable. He didn't really have a woman in his life, thus he was constantly horny. Certainly not a romantic partner. He had Celine and Angela, of course, but even though he adored them, that did nothing to improve his love life.

At the time James arrived to Connelly's and waited by the door for the others to come, he was feeling a bit anxious. When she arrived first and kissed his cheek, Angela gave him some relief.

"Okay, I apologize for being a little harsh with you the last time. Whether or if you slept with Kelly is none of my business."

"I'm grateful you were honest with me, but your ideas are still important to me."

But you don't concur with me, she remarked with a smile.

Also grinning, He admitted, "I admit that I initially didn't. I thought it was because Kelly and I are both unmarried. But that disregards other information. Things that both Celine and you made me think of.

Celine and Austin had just gotten there and were saying hello when Kelly showed up. James gave her a smile and wrapped his arms around her as they kissed lightly. They all grinned as they quickly evaluated this older woman who had entered their world and generated so much discussion as he made the introductions. As they entered, James noticed that his arm was around Kelly's waist and, much to Angela's surprise, made a point of doing the same with her. He only grinned sweetly at her as she turned to face him. He reasoned that by putting his arm around Angela, he would be able to diffuse the issue and avoid having to later defend himself to his friends about Kelly and him being more than friends. He was obviously mistaken.

CHAPTER 13

Kelly was aware that James's pals were having a look at her, but she had anticipated it and, to some part, understood. She was aware that they were aware of their previous liaisons, but she was unaware of the specifics and was also unaware that they had recently had intimate moments. While she was grinning, the others were oblivious to the fact that her feelings and thoughts extended much beyond simply getting to know James's buddies. James's decision to visit Kelly once more made her feel wonderful. Kelly, who is 41 years old, attracted a young man who was in his peak sexually, and the two of them screwed till they were immobile. Then once more, twice. Just a few days prior, he had visited her once more and slept in her bed. She was aware that James had contributed to her reluctance to commit to her elder friend and lover. He was good, but James was so much better that she questioned whether she could find a younger man to marry. James is younger, but this might be a compromise. She genuinely wanted that. She liked James a lot, but she wanted to get married to a man who could satisfy her sex demands and desires.

For his part, James sat back and tried to observe how the others interacted and discussed topics other than sex and relationships. All of them meeting Kelly was his idea, and it had happened. However, he had time to sit there and contrast Kelly with Angela and Celine before he realized it. There was a clear and noticeable age difference. Kelly's perception of the world and her responses to various comments changed, not because she appeared older, though that too became more obvious. Kelly was a wise woman who was young for her years, but more in terms of appearance than outlook. In fact, the changes were so striking that when he reached over to take Angela's hand while Celine was speaking to Kelly, she gave him a short glance. After giving her a brief smile and gentle squeeze, James let go of her hand. He needed Angela to know something, but he couldn't tell her what he was thinking. Even he wasn't certain. He simply understood the need for Angela to be aware of his continued friendship with his pals.

He tried to understand the message Angela was sending him after she reciprocated his squeeze, but he was unable to do so. Just knowing that she didn't mind him being there or being there made me feel better.

Later, as they exited the restaurant, they stood outside and exchanged thank-you and goodbyes. No one mentioned repeating the event, and James didn't see any justification for doing so either.

When James discovered Angela was following him home instead of turning to go to her apartment, she was more than a mile from the restaurant. Oh sh*t, she's got something on her mind, he thought. It was still early in the evening, so as long as they could converse maturely while sipping wine, everything would be OK. He just didn't feel like arguing or having lengthy moral debates.

When she exited her car while grinning at him, he had the opportunity to kiss her. He could now unwind, and perhaps they could both enjoy each other's company.

She asked him, "Surprised?" after she joined him after he waited.

"Yes, but this is fantastic. Does wine sound appetizing?

"Yes, it does, but not a lot."

I already have a couple splits, so I'm good to go. No more trouble for me, right?

Although you're not in danger, you must feel guilty.

You have to acknowledge that this is incredibly unique, yet not at all.

Although it is unusual, what does it matter? He was unable to respond to that.

Following him to his little kitchen, Angela observed him take two splits of Blue Nun wine. 'Great,' I think this is great.

"This Reisling is good."

He sat across from her on the loveseat while Angela led the way into the living room and sat at the end of the couch.

James, are you and Kelly taking your relationship more seriously now?

Why do you ask that, I hear you cry, "Hell no, of course not."

"Because you're seated over there, clearly."

I didn't want you to think that, though.

I didn't want to give you the wrong impression, after all.

I'll simply relocate there.

Okay, sit at the end here. She lied, saying, "I believe that's kind of a man thing. She sat down next to him after he sat down and commented, "That's much better, now we can talk better."

Are we going to discuss tonight's dinner or Kelly and her?

Not exactly, unless you feel the need to say something.

What did you think of her, then?

"Very good and attractive, just like you mentioned. I absolutely concur with your taste and your evaluation of her, with one exception. She is 44 years old, yet she doesn't appear any younger. Sure, she looks nice, but not so nice.

"You know, I have to admit that I now mostly concur with you. For some reason, tonight, I had a different perception of her. She may not seem as young as I had imagined, but she still appears young for her age.

Alright, question. Why did you keep silent over dinner?

"Well, I thought I'd be quiet and let the three of you converse because I wanted the three of you to meet her. In addition, I was attempting to examine my thoughts and feelings toward Kelly. In case you missed it, I'm a little lost. Perhaps how she would approach me had some affect on me.

"Perhaps that's connected in some way. Additionally, you might be a little sexually unsatisfied or deprived, but I have no idea.

I appreciate it; I feel lot more macho now.

Oh, don't take anything too seriously. We all experience that once in a while, but I believe men do so far more frequently than women. Okay, I have a new query. Let's make that a series of questions. When we entered the restaurant, why did you choose to wrap your arm around mine?

"I assume you'd prefer I refrain from doing that."

"Avoid drawing hasty conclusions. I can't help but be curious because you don't usually do that.

Actually, I was holding Kelly in my other arm, I admit.

"Yes, I saw that,"

I admit that I didn't stop doing that until it was too late. I was concerned that you and the other people might take things too far.

You wrapped your arm around me in order to prevent any erroneous inferences from being made.

"That's accurate."

"You know, that doesn't really make me look good. To sort of throw everyone off the track, you were using me.

"Damn, I'm not going to win. We're all friends, so we've always avoided that difficulty, but if I had stated I had your arm around you because you were so great and so appealing that I couldn't resist you, I'd be in trouble.

Which is the truth, then?

The first statement is accurate, but I'd also like to point you that I didn't mind putting my arm around you.

"You were unbothered. Therefore, if I had been your sister, the meaning would have been similar.

CHAPTER 14

I never said that. Why are you attempting to stir up a fight so hard?

I'm not; I'm only looking for the truth.

"I told you the truth, and you were angry about it."

"How about you take hold of my hand and squeeze it? That was probably only for show and had no significance to you, too.

Even though I squeezed your hand in return,

Okay, but you didn't respond to my query.

I wanted to squeeze your hand, so I did. I was attempting to express my gratitude for your presence.

"Is that all?"

Well, what else could it possibly mean?

"I'm not sure,"

Why then did you grip my hand in response?

As a result of my desire. Since I was thanking you and felt that was a nice gesture.

Where is this all taking us?

"I was moving in that direction. I still had a question for you. Are you attempting to rekindle our relationship?

James was becoming perplexed and lost. Why would I act in such way?

That was perhaps the worst thing James could have said, in my opinion.

"It is what I said is an excellent question. Along with Celine and Austin, we have known each other for about twenty years. Why do you assume I'm hitting on you all of a sudden just because I encircled you with my arm and squeezed your hand? That justification is pretty flimsy.

Well, I can't help it; everything there was so novel to me that I had to ask that.

Do you feel more secure knowing that I'm not making advances toward you now?

I always feel safe with you and the others, she said after pausing for a brief moment. I feel secure, cherished, and at ease. Okay, so perhaps I reacted too strongly.

"After all this time, what triggered that?"

That's my argument. After all this time, those events finally occurred.

"Hold on, I just realized something. You rested your head on my leg while I was telling my tale while you watched. Do you think that, along with the fact that my hand was resting on your belly, in any way contributed to this?

"No of course not. I told you then that I liked it and I felt so loved and comfortable, just like I said a minute ago and that's all. You said you enjoyed that."

"I really did. You looked so nice and so serene lying there. Wait. Lie on the couch with your head on my thigh like you did that night."

She changed her position and then his arm went around and his hand landed onto her belly. "I wanted to see what I missed that night." Her top had pulled up enough that most of his hand was on her warm belly, but neither of them commented on that minor detail. He looked down at her and asked, "Was it sort of like this?"

"Pretty much. Okay, while we're like this, can you think of an old story that you could tell me. Maybe a short one."

Had she been paying closer attention, she would have noticed that his smile had a devilish quality to it as he began his tale. "Do you remember when we were about ten and that Mrs. Dominic that lived in that little white house behind me?"

"I haven't thought of her in years, but I sort of remember her. What about her?"

"Do you remember the Carpenters that lived on the corner?"

"Sure, I used to play with Tracy, their daughter."

"That's the ones. Well, one day when I was playing in the yard, Mr. Carpenter came down the little alley between your house and mine and went toward Mrs. Dominic's and he was carrying a tiny cluster of flowers. That got my curiosity going so I followed him. I didn't know about sex or any of that at that point, so I had no preconceived ideas. I do remember Mom and Dad talking about Mrs. Carpenter being such a sour pussed prude and she never smiled, but that's all I remember about her. Her grumpy face and she was always looking straight ahead. Anyway, Nathan

Carpenter went down that alley and right to Mrs. Dominic's house, handed her the flowers and she quickly looked around to see if they had been seen and then pulled him inside and closed the door.

She was looking up at him with a hint of a smile as she asked, "Are you sure you remember this correctly?"

"I'm sure."

"Okay, so what about all of that, what happened?"

"Well, I went around to the side of the house and that turned out to be her bedroom."

"My god James, you were peeping."

"That's right, but at that time and at the age of ten I don't think I would have been sent to jail or to a shrink. I wanted to see why Mr. Carpenter was going to see a neighbor woman when he was already married. Well I got an education for my efforts."

She was smiling up at him now as she imagined him stretching to see over the window sill. "James you were being so bad."

"To me, I was being so curious and inquisitive. I didn't realize that I was going to get a visual lesson in procreating."

Again she smiled as she told him, "Thank you for using that word. Sorry, keep going."

"Um...Angela, I'll do my best to keep it as clean as I can. I watched tall Mr. Carpenter undress the shorter and heavier Mrs. Dominic and she did all she could to make it easy for him."

CHAPTER 15

"Wasn't Mrs. Dominic quite a bit older than he was?"

"Yeah, but I don't know by how much. Anyway, before they got into bed he had his hands all over her and then he...he knelt down in front of her. I guess I'll let you fill in the blanks."

'It's okay, tell me."

"Okay. He went between her legs and ate her until I thought she would be sick, because I heard what were to me at the time, some weird sounds coming from her. She stopped him and undressed him and that's the first time I ever saw an erect adult...penis." Angela was smiling and no longer interrupting him now as he went on. "Well they screwed, Angela. Him on top, her on top and him behind her, and then some... I don't remember exactly, but one of the side positions. I really didn't care because in the process, I saw her pus...between her legs and I saw her big pendulous breasts as he buried his face in them. They kissed and to me at the time, it looked like they were trying to swallow each other.

Angela chuckled at that one but she waited for him to continue.

"Angela... It made me so...well erect that it scared me. I mean I'd had that happen a couple of times before, but this time I didn't think it would ever go away and that scared me until I remembered listening to some of the older boys talking about their cocks...sorry. Well you know."

"That's okay James, I know about cocks, but thank you."

"Well I didn't wait for them to dress. I slipped back to the alley and raced home and hid until I was soft again. I was so relieved when that happened, but I couldn't stop thinking about what I'd seen for a couple of days."

"So you really did get an education."

"Oh yes I really did."

"James, the reason I wanted you to tell me a story was I wanted to see if you'd caress me again."

He looked down at her hand and her top was pushed up enough that his whole hand was on her belly and even under her top slightly. His first instinct was to jerk it away, but instead, he looked at her and said, "I'm sorry Angela, why didn't you stop me?"

"It feels good and I wanted to see if you'd realize what you were doing. I didn't put my hand on yours to stop you because I didn't want to draw your attention to it. James, it's just my belly. You don't try to move up to my breasts or whatever, so it's just a sweet gesture, just like I said the last time." She didn't move as she smiled up at him and asked, "Now you didn't make that up about Mrs. Dominic did you?"

"I promise I did not. It turned out that she entertained more than one husband in the neighborhood."

"She didn't."

"She did, and I never could understand why. She wasn't great looking and she was overweight."

"She was also willing and I'd even guess pretty good in bed. That was very dangerous for her to do that right in her own neighborhood, but I guess she got away with it."

"I guess she did."

"Okay James, now why did you choose that story to tell me?"

"That was what popped into my mind first. That and I considered making up a story, but I liked the idea of one from your childhood better. Besides, I thought that had a touch of romance, a touch of sex and deception and it was short. Not enough to be included in a book of short stories, but not too bad."

She put her hand on his and felt it press against her belly as she looked up at him. Then she pushed his hand away and sat up.

"Okay Angela so you've proved that I do caress your belly, so does that mean you won't put your head on my thigh again?"

"Of course not, I told you I liked that, and I liked it this time as well. I'll bet Celine would like it too."

"Okay, tomorrow night, while Austin tells his story, I'll ask her to be with me."

"She'll ask questions at the least."

"Maybe I can tell her I'm conducting some research."

"Or you could tell her the truth."

"Maybe that would be the better option."

"Just don't get any wild ideas and do anything funny."

"Funny how?"

CHAPTER 16

"You know, move your hands almost to where they shouldn't be and pretend you're not aware of what you're doing."

"Very funny, had I had that idea it would have happened to you minutes ago."

"Oh, so you did consider that."

"Not until you mentioned it just now love."

"I'm going home. I'll be here on time tomorrow night and I expect to have a very entertaining night. Both from Austin's story and from watching you with Celine."

"I'm looking forward to that too."

"Oh is that right."

"Of course, now I'll compare bellies and see if she reacts to me differently than you did."

They got up and he followed her to the door where she turned around and smiled just before she kissed him and let her tongue just touch his lips before she pulled back. "That's for telling me a story James. Night," and he watched her go down the two steps.

"Hey pretty one," and she stopped and turned around. "Thanks. Thanks for coming over and for the kiss. It's been great."

Thank you, night," she said as she climbed inside her vehicle. He locked the door after watching her walk out and leave. He grinned as he made his way back to the living room, where he paused to reflect on their conversation. He was eagerly anticipating Austin's narrative, Celine's response to his request, and tomorrow night.

James's first party included Austin, and as James finished up his own take on cheese and olive appetizers, the two of them chatted in the kitchen. They're nothing spectacular, but beer would pair well with them.

They had their first round of nibbles and their first bottles of beer as soon as Angela and Celine arrived. They then proceeded to the living room with freshly opened bottles that had been poured into frosty mugs. Celine went over and sat down on the loveseat after noticing Angela was going to sit close to Austin.

"Why don't you join me on the floor," James remarked as he leaned down to speak to her. He remarked, "If you're willing, I'd want to have you sleep with your head on my leg like Angela did the previous time," before she had a chance to respond.

With a smile, she enquired, "So James, what are you up to?"

How should I describe this?

That's what I'm waiting to find out, hon, she remarked with a hint of laughter.

As Angela and I were discussing it, I thought, "Hell, I just want to see whether, when I get immersed in Austin's narrative, my hand starts to rub your tummy, and if it happens, what you'll say or think and all of that."

"So, you're testing things out."

"Exactly, and I told Angela that, but she said I should be more honest about it," she remarked.

Okay lover boy, settle in, but first let me sip a bit of my beer while Austin tells his tale.

The two of them were seated very close to one another, and Austin began, "My story begins when I was about fourteen or fifteen. I believe it was fifteen. Anyway, I cried like I was being murdered when Mom said that we would be attending the family reunion. Since it wouldn't be long until school started and we wanted to use our inline skates, I wanted to be with my buddies. Additionally, Fred Napsy discovered his father's collection of girly magazines, which made us eager to get some fresh ones out of the home so we could go hide and examine them. Celine and Angela grinned at him but held their comments.

Anyway, Mom told us not to argue because everyone was going and that everyone's relatives would be there, Austin said. Sandra Grahams, my cousin, came to mind, which made it easier for me to quit complaining. Although no one knew, she and I had a great time together the summer before, and I was still smitten with her.

What age were you when you first developed feelings for her, Angela said, "maybe thirteen or fourteen? What was her age?

"Maybe thirteen," I'm not sure. But she was incredibly cute—I mean incredibly—cute. She also let me to feel and run my fingers through her amazing long golden hair, which sparkled in the sun and had me fascinated. Anyway, I stopped talking after that and started counting down the days until that Saturday morning when we attended the reunion.

The reunion would be held at my uncle Reese's farm, which was enormous and had enormous barns and what looked like miles of Scott, Austin added after taking a big swig of beer. We were instructed not to get on the enormous tractors and to avoid the barns. Of course, those were only the locations we were most eager to visit.

Celine placed her wet cup on the coaster, sat down, and made herself comfortable with her head resting on James's thigh while gazing up at him with a smile. However, she remained silent. She tilted her head to look at Austin as his tale went on.

Well, Sandra Grahams wasn't there, and I was upset enough to be on the verge of fleeing.

James's hand was already on Celine's exposed midriff beneath her baggy top before Angela noticed it, but she didn't say anything or even establish eye contact with either of them. He needed to be conscious of his actions. She knew it just by looking at the placement of his hand—under rather than on top of her top.

Austin was stating, "So there Sandra Grahams was and as soon as she spotted me she grinned and ran over to me," while Angela was thinking about that. Damn, just the thought that she was so happy to see me made me feel better. We started conversing after she inquired about how I was doing and didn't stop until my cousin Carl and his companion joined us. Well, that put an end to everything between Sandra Grahams and me, and although I wanted to get rid of the others, it was unlikely to happen. My gaze would frequently wander to her legs while the four of us sat on the grass in the shade. She was wearing hot pink short shorts and a shortie top, and I vividly recall swooning at the sight of them. I was, however, acting as though I was engaged in what the others were saying. The best we could manage was a single touch of her thigh and a smile from each other. Then, as Sandra Grahams placed her hand on my arm and someone yelled, "There's ice cream," Carl and his friend, whose name I cannot recall, leaped to their feet. Sandra Grahams tugged on my arm as the other two hurried off, and I followed her to a tiny structure where we disappeared from view. We could spend as much time by ourselves as we wanted.

While James was listening to the narrative, Celine was looking up at him, and he was gently circling her stomach with his palm. She had been assured by Angela that it was pleasant and comforting, and it was. However, there was more. To be certain, it wasn't a sexual gesture. But to her, it was sensual. Despite being soft from office labor, his hands didn't feel anything like hers. Additionally, she could feel his thumb delicately brush her bra through her breasts. He would do this repeatedly. As far as advancements go, that would have to be ranked as weak and wimpy at best, and she actually laughed at herself at one point. He wasn't even glancing her way, though. Additionally, those minor sensations kept happening repeatedly. Small tics kept telling her that his hand was on her lower chest, soft abdomen, and under her top. She could hear Austin's voice, but she frequently closed her eyes. She was at her happiest at that very moment. She once more experienced what Angela had described, feeling warm, cherished, and at ease with everyone and everything.

Her thoughts were interrupted once more by Austin's voice, who said, "By ducking from building to building we were soon out of sight so we could relax and just walk around anywhere we wanted to travel. I took her hand in mine as we continued walking so closely together that we occasionally bumped into one another, smiled, and continued walking. Looking back, there was a risk we might get lost, but we didn't consider that possibility at the time. I still ponder what might have happened on that particular day if we had been older. My feelings for her were so strong they filled my entire being.

Angela remarked, "Time for a break, and a fresh drink," and she quickly left for the restroom.

Celine was on her belly and James was softly massaging his hands over her partially exposed back when Austin stepped out from the kitchen. Although James said, "Oh god, that feels so great, thank you," he didn't interpret that as a command to stop. Before leaving, Angela noticed James's hand moving up her back, letting her know that he was gently caressing Celine while his hand was on or just past her bra strap. Angela hurried swiftly to join Austin as her cheeks began to slightly flush.

I hate to stop, but I need to follow Angela's lead, Celine finally said. She stood up, gave James a thank-you kiss, and then left to use the restroom. Just before Celine arrived, James dashed to his bedroom, used the restroom, and then dashed to the kitchen. Celine's breasts were swaying beneath her plain tee shirt, making it difficult for Angela to miss the fact that her bra was unhooked. Although it could still be seen, Celine's bra was not helping to support her breasts. Angela averted her eyes as she took a sizable swig from her open beer bottle. Her beer was going down too quickly, so she wouldn't need another mug of frost.

Austin, I adore your story, Celine replied.

"I'm grateful. It undoubtedly triggers some vivid recollections.

"I'm willing to bet it does, and I can't wait to see how it turns out." Angela said, "I'm ready to hear more," and she returned to the living room empty handed. She didn't need another beer, though. If Austin's tale included a depressing section and she had consumed significantly more wine, she would be sniffling and crying. She couldn't allow herself to feel that ashamed.

After Austin joined her, Celine and James took up their previous places. Celine was once more on her back as James sat on the floor with his back to the loveseat. Had she adjusted the bra hooks? Angela simply couldn't be certain.

CHAPTER 17

When Angela looked at Austin, who had moved a bit closer to her, he simply grinned and said, "Okay, back to Sandra Grahams. We kept holding hands as our feet led us along an ancient path where my uncle used to walk the dairy animals.

She remarked, "Oh nuts Austin, we can't go any farther," when we eventually reached an old barbed wire fence.

"Yes, we can; allow me to demonstrate a trick." In order to hold down the bottom strand as I tugged the other one up and said, "See, now you can slip through," I took off my shirt and tied it around it.

But what about my back? Those pointy objects will be right up against it.

"You'll be fine if you just move carefully,"

I've got a better idea," she said as she casually lifted her shirt over her head and covered the top strand with it. She slipped through while grinning at me as I watched her breasts and bra, and I immediately did the same. She then removed her top from the fence while watching me do the same. She then turned and resumed her stroll while holding her top in an upended position. After that, I was such a huge mess. Instead of holding hands as we walked, I wrapped my arm around her and pulled her close. Although it wasn't simple, neither of us wanted to give up the sensation of her warm flesh caressing mine and vice versa. We estimated that only our head and shoulders would be visible above the crops as we were edging a soybean field because the path was heavily rutted from the cows and the tall, green soybeans. When Sandra Grahams realized this, she first removed her shorts before removing mine and handing them to me. Sorry, gals, but I have to admit that I remained as stern as those fence posts because I kept staring at her small underwear spread across her gorgeous butt.

Celine's breasts' bottoms were discovered by James's thumb as his hand circled around under her blouse once more. Although it wasn't enough to even suggest he was touching them, it was enough to constantly bringing up how near he was to actually touching them. His delicate fingers moved without any resistance because her bra was unsecured. His thumb lightly brushed the undersides of both breasts. First one, then the other a minute later, then down a little lower and over her tummy before rising again Celine went from being quite relaxed and a little fuzzy-headed to being highly attentive and receptive to his every touch. Only if his hand actually grabbed her breast under her top would she genuinely stop him from continuing. Even if the other two were in their secure place, if they weren't present, she still would have invited them. Despite the fact that she was fully awake, James seemed to be casting her into a trance. She turned to face Austin when he halted, but he and Angela had only just slightly adjusted their postures.

CHAPTER 18

When I remarked, "Let's turn around and go back up a few ways," Sandra Grahams made a point of glancing at my erection.

She asked me, "You want to go back to the picnic?" with an expression of surprise.

"No, I've got a better place in mind."

She grinned and managed to brush her palm across my cock as we turned around.

" Austin wasn't being as careful with his words as James was as his story grew more personal and sensual.

"That's when she gave me a kiss. She gave me a heartfelt kiss, and when my hands reached for her bra strap after that, I could feel her stop moving. Looking back, that was fairly amusing since we were still lips-to-lips and, I don't think, neither of us was even breathing. However, my trembling hands managed to remove the hooks, and we then started breathing normally.

Austin paused and turned to look at Celine and James before turning back to Angela, who appeared absorbed in his tale. As they waited for James to speak, James's hand was still on Celine beneath her blouse, but it was no longer moving.

I removed her bra and held it in my hands while we ceased kissing and turned to face each other. Sandra Grahams remained still as I fixed my gaze on her breasts and stared at them for a moment before I dared to touch one of them. I believed that when I died,

I was going to heaven. At that young age, breasts are extraordinarily firm, as we all know, and I was in love; I just knew that I was. Then they were like... as I touched her nipple. I can't come up with a useful comparison. They too were quite tough and protruded from her breasts. She practically murmured, "We best stroll for a while," as she stopped me at that point. The last thing I wanted to do was that. However, because we had to move, I took us back to the barn that was the furthest from the picnic. We entered via the partially closed door and continued past the tractor. She went first, and I followed after showing her the wooden ladder that led up a post and to the hayloft. Because my face was only a few inches away from her amazing ass and her little underwear, I was the luckiest guy in the world that day. When James imagined Sandra Grahams's tight, sweet, virginal ass covered in tiny underwear, his hand began to move on its own. The events in Austin's story were having an impact on Celine as well, but she was still conscious of James's sly hand caressing the lower corners of her breasts after it had snuck under her bra. Every time that happened, she tried to coerce his hand to reach a little bit higher, but it always remained that playful, almost innocent caress.

As Austin continued his story, he stated, "I was going insane. "I kissed her rapidly, pressing my lips to her butt, and that stopped her. She clung on the ladder while I kept giving her a stupid little kiss on the behind. I was enjoying myself, and I imagine she did too. Then I really pushed my luck and, while still hanging on, I pulled her pants down so that I could kiss her left ass cheek. I watched her as she continued to climb the ladder until she could get down and onto the hay bales after saying, "Oh god." We didn't tumble off and land on that tractor, which surprises me. As our arms around one another, we essentially had the feeling that we were in our own little apartment or bedroom. Particularly as I kissed her and my left hand reached the top of her underwear, we were both dangerously near to losing what little control we still had. She didn't stop me this time either, so I knelt down and carefully exposed her most private information as I pushed her pants down and she exited them. I was gazing at and kissing my Sandra Grahams when she was completely naked. I wanted to cry as she stopped me from reaching for her breasts once more. I simply knew that she was going to get dressed and that she was afraid.

Angela remained motionless as she waited for him to finish since she was so engrossed in his story. Celine remained unchanged, and James's hand essentially stopped moving as well. Only Celine's right breast was teased as his thumb slowly moved back and forth under her bra.

Austin recalled, "Instead of stopping, she bent down and gradually tugged my underwear down to my ankles. I remained still. She stared at me as she declared, "I've never seen a real one before," and for once he avoided saying cock and simply replied,

"Started at me. She touched me after that, and I can still feel my insides shivering now. I was losing my mind. If my life had been on the line right then, I wouldn't have been able to think clearly or sensibly. We ended up lying on hay bales, oblivious to the dry, green, and scratchy hay's prodding and sticking.

I promptly consented to her request that I make a pledge not to enter her. At that moment, I was willing to agree to whatever she could think of. In order to feel each other with our entire bodies, we explored and laid down. We kissed, chatted, and continued our exploration. I'll never forget how it felt to have her hands all over me and how she felt when they were on her. She even used her mouth to force me," he began, but stopped himself and added, "Well, you understand what I mean."

That's my narrative, Austin stated as he turned to face Angela and appeared to be speaking only to her.

That was an amazing story, Austin, Angela replied while grinning and leaning over to give him a quick kiss. She muttered, "Damn you," and then grinned once more. Even if he understood what she was saying, he only grinned at her before turning to face the other two.

Celine exclaimed, "That was so nice and amazing, thank you Austin," as James's palm finally settled on her belly at the waistband of her shorts.

"Thank you very much."

"But then, what happened? You understand at the picnic, right?

CHAPTER 19

Sandra Grahams and I had chunks of that blasted hay in our clothes, and we were covered in scratches and poke marks from it. We almost panicked when we heard our names being called, but we were able to get dressed and almost fall down the ladder as we hurried to get away. The barn once served as our bedroom, but now it may turn into a trap. We were able to get away from the situation far enough so that we had time to check ourselves and each other, cleaning off any hay particles we discovered. We were standing there in the lane naked and were quite close to restarting things. She then gave me her underwear as a gift after giving me another kiss. When we came home, both my parents gave me grief, and they pressed and interrogated me for days after that, but I stuck to my half-truths. We took a very long walk, but Sandra Grahams and I didn't hear them calling. They never accepted the explanations I gave for the scratches on my body. When Sandra Grahams and I were playing horse and fighting in the back hay field, I said it came from the weeds.

"I'm going to assume you still have her underwear."

Yes, I still have her underwear, he chuckled.

Do you see her often anymore, Angela questioned?

"We don't get together very frequently, but when we do, we try to find some alone time to go through those memories and that entire period of our life. She still claims to have loved me deeply at the time. She asks me if I shared her sentiments.

However, did you really?

"Yes, I did—at least, that's how I recall it. Even now, after only seeing her a few times a year, those emotions still resurface, but not as strongly as they did back then. In my heart, she will always have a very special place.

Austin, we're seeing your romantic side and I enjoy that, Angela added with a smile. We appreciate you sharing with us.

I hope I didn't get carried away too much.

You did well. At such a tender and innocent stage in your life, I could nearly sense the intensity of your experience. I'm sure you're innocent up until that point.

I'm with Angela, that was very nice and sensual, and thank you for sharing, Celine added as she turned to face Austin.

"I'm happy you enjoyed it. What about your narrative, Celine?

"Hear me out about my story. I don't want to leave our evening on a depressing note, but I've been thinking about it, and it's not a happy one. Let's completely forget about it, in fact.

Celine, hold on a second, James commanded. We spoke about important events in our lives. Not joyful, sexy, or romantic, but important. We all value this moment because it is so meaningful to you. That doesn't mean our evening has to come to an end there. We're all still young and capable, so what does it matter if we stay up a bit longer talking? Please let us know. If it's essential to you, it must also be important to us. And who knows, perhaps discussing it with us will help you push it so far back into your memory that it won't cross your mind ever again.

You're correct, James, Celine murmured as she turned to face him. Like Angela mentioned, lying here makes me feel very cherished. When will I be able to confront it if not now?

As he drew her closer to him, James's hand crept under her top and up her back. One thing is certain, honey; we will all love you and support you to the very end. He gave her a tender kiss and said.

He was tightly held in her arms as she embraced him and said, "Thank you, James. Can I once more use your leg as a pillow and you as a support?

"I'm hoping you'll."

"One more thing: I enjoy the feel of your hands on me, especially when they are on my naked back. Thank you also for it.

"I do adore that too."

Okay, I need to go the restroom, have a few of snacks, and have another drink for strength before I begin my narrative," Celine stated as she stood up and James's hand slipped out from beneath her blouse.

Angela said, "Me too," and went into the bathroom behind her, closing the door behind her. We need to talk for a moment, Celine.

"Sure," you say.

CHAPTER 20

"I know this is a touchy subject, but don't you think James has a little too much freedom?"

What are you saying?

By using his hand. He has really been examining you, in my opinion.

I can tell you precisely where his hand has been, and I don't mind.

But isn't it letting him touch your breasts...

I am concerned about how that may affect our informal gatherings.

Celine remarked, "His hands haven't been on my breasts, Angela," as she turned to face her.

But see how your bra is unhooked—his hand had to be there.

On my breasts, please. My bra is unhooked, well, whatever. I had him unhook my bra as he was massaging, rubbing, or otherwise rubbing my back so he could move freely and his hand wouldn't be pressing against my bra strap. Nothing to worry about.

But it's not hooked yet.

When Celine realized she was getting a little irritable, she stated, "I have a remedy for that," and she removed her top, followed by her bra, before putting her top back on. That's better, I see.

That's not what I meant, Celine.

"See Angela, I enjoyed having my bra unhooked. Being liberated and more at ease made me feel happy. In fact, I might not wear

a bra the following time. Are you envious of what James and I are sharing, Angela?

Of course not Celine, I just don't want the dynamics between the four of us to change.

"Angela, change is the only constant in life. Each of us is evolving. Although we cannot stop it, we can try to change it on our own or adapt to it. In either case, change is a constant in our world. While we're talking about it, one more thing. When I begin my story, I'll go back to James immediately. Although it won't be simple for me and will actually make me feel beyond embarrassed, I'm going forward with it thanks to your encouragement as well as that of Austin and James. I'm going to talk about it openly in the hopes that it will leave my thoughts. Are you certain Angela that you are not envious?

Naturally, I'm certain. Okay, I apologize; perhaps I have overreacted.

Or perhaps Austin's tale was starting to affect you a little.

Yes, of course it did, but I'm sure it affected you as well.

"Not at first, but when I tell you my tale, I'm sure you'll understand all of that," she said.

When the women arrived, Austin and James were in the kitchen. The four of them drank another beer and nibbled on the goodies while conversing. Celine was now braless, and both boys noticed it, but they kept quiet. She didn't have a bra, and it was certain that it wasn't in one of her pockets, so James pondered where it was. He had to question her decision as well. Did she think he would accept further information? He was reluctant to put that to the test, particularly in front of the other two. He emptied his bottle and went in search of another one because he was now anxious. He resisted doing two things. Both of them involved getting an erection once they were back in the living room and his hand was close to her now-almost-unhindered breasts. The first involved assuming incorrectly that she wanted him to do more only to have her reject him. Either of those would be really embarrassing.

Well, the tougher it will be for me to convey my story the longer I wait, Celine added after finishing her beer. Since James's beer bottle was still largely full, he had it with him as the four of them moved to the living room and settled down once more. This time, James sat on the floor opposite from Angela and leaned on the loveseat while Austin sat at the end of the couch with Angela sitting on the ground between his feet. Celine grinned up at him as she sat down, reclined, and put her head back on his leg. While Angela and Austin watched them, she grabbed his hand in hers, put it beneath her top, and laid it on her tummy before he could react.

I'll warn you right now that I will probably cry at some point of this story, Celine remarked, still looking up at James. Before returning to Angela and his seat on the sofa, Austin stood up, ran to the restroom, and pulled out a box of tissues, placing them on the floor next to her. That was good, Austin, she murmured as she tilted her head back and raised her eyes.

Celine turned to face them and said, "It was Austin, and thank you. I have to go back a long way, so please be patient as I explain a few things first, she said after taking a deep breath. I had to be no older than twelve. I was probably around twelve, maybe thirteen. I had just begun to blossom. You're familiar with tiny breast bumps and other things. I was still a wild child who enjoyed running and chasing and acting both like a boy and a girl, but the inevitable was gradually taking place. The lads began to perceive me as more of a girl as I began to like the girlie things and dabble with makeup. I enjoyed it, but at the same time, I frequently was not invited to participate in some of the games with the boys because I was a lady. I suppose a turning moment. But as time went on—I'm talking a matter of months at most—I become completely feminine. My brother was no longer permitted to enter my room unless I specifically requested him, things like that. And if he caught me in my underwear, I was traumatized. I even didn't want my father to see me in my underwear.

I remember how it was too Celine, Angela remarked with a little smile. I would go from being a tomboy and raising hell to being in my room experimenting with new makeup and getting dressed while I modeled in the mirror.

CHAPTER 21

"Exactly. Anyway, I grew down there and my breasts developed very quickly.

Celine, if you're trying to say pubic hair, just say pubic hair and whatever else comes up, James told her as he stopped her. We're all adults, and trying to be kind and sensitive will only make it more difficult for you to relate your tale. Just be open, okay? Austin said "cock" a couple times, but we made it through that.

My pubic hair seemed to appear over night," she stated, giving the others a quick glance before turning to focus more on the ceiling. It was first light in hue and downy, but I was captivated by it for a long. Even though I was trying to trim mine into a pattern, I looked at some photos of naked ladies. A diamond once, then a straightforward strip—sorry, I'm getting off track. Okay, so Dad frequently invaded my personal space and would catch me in my underwear or, worse, while I was completely naked. I'm not sure how often he glanced at my developing breasts and the space in between my legs. One day, in a little huff, he claimed that even as I grew, there was nothing wrong with him seeing me naked because I was his tiny daughter. I gave up arguing with him and simply ignored his unexpected visits after that. Dad was always there for me when things got difficult at school or when I got into a quarrel with a buddy as life continued. Even when I was in my underwear or completely naked, he would hold me close to him and touch my back and butt, as if he were frightened he might lose me or something. He simply didn't give a damn. I tried to convince myself that he cared about me and that he loved me, but that didn't account for his...erections. For a very long time, I pretended that I was making it up or that his hardness was due to anything else. Perhaps he and Mom had been having fun. He also caressed my breasts a few times while he inquired about bras. Did they fit, did I need new ones, larger ones, and such such things."

Despite knowing where this was going, they all found it hard to trust what they were hearing. Her father struck James, Austin, and Angela as a genuinely nice man while they were still able to recall him. Always willing to serve as their pitcher or repair a backstop. The kids seemed to make him happy to be there.

With his free hand, James lightly caressed her face and enquired, "You okay, love?"

She gave him a thank-you kiss on the hand as she proceeded while grinning up at him and simply nodding. I'm not sure how much you remember, but Dad and Mom were divorced and he moved into a townhouse. Mom cried a lot, and I was oblivious to the reasons for their breakup, but I never overheard her criticizing him. She would find a way to ignore my questions or simply tell me not to worry that everything would be well. After that, I only saw Dad on weekends when Mom or aunt Frieda were around. Every once in a while, Mom and I would visit

Uncle Norm, where they would chat as I strolled around the tiny woods behind his home. I enjoyed it outside. There was a lot to look into and learn about. I suppose that while I was there, my tomboy side returned. I was still captivated by the simple things, like the tiny brook in the back that trickled through some rocks, even though I didn't want to get dirty because I was still a girl.

I believe I remember your uncle Norm, Austin said to the woman.

You most likely do. On one occasion, when my mother would leave me there with Uncle Norm for a whole weekend, I got a sliver in my butt. It had to be removed, either by Uncle Norm or the doctor, and he informed me that if the doctor did it, he would give me a shot once he had pulled the sliver out. It hurt so bad that it made me weep. A shot was pretty much the last thing I wanted, so I gulped and agreed he may administer it. He told me that he needed to be able to see the sliver and make sure it wasn't becoming infected, so he took down both my shorts and my underwear as well. I couldn't believe it at the time. I naturally didn't realize an infection couldn't spread so quickly, so I gave in.

Angela exclaimed, "Oh goodness, that had to be difficult to go through."

It initially was, but he was so kind and kind, and I had spent so much time with him and out there that it didn't seem any worse to me than having my father see me. Of course, I have to go by how I recall it. Anyway, because Mom worked during the day and Uncle Norm started working at midnight, I started spending more and more time at his house. I can still clearly recall the first time I saw him naked. He explained it by adding that one of his problems was that he was so warm. He would become overheated and uncomfortable when other individuals might be at ease. Naturally, I assured him that I was fine. Since it was his home, he had a right to feel at ease. I wasn't concerned at the time, except from almost seeing his cock. He would sit next to me while we watched a movie on television, doing nothing more than talking to each other. Uncle Norm's cock was considerably more noticeable through the thin cotton of his underwear than Dad's, which I remembered to be occasionally hard.

One day he asked Celine, "Celine, have your parents discussed sex with you?"

I was unable to look at him because my heart was racing. Had he noticed that I was glancing at his erection? "Not quite,"

They used to refer to it as "birds and bees talk," but I believe you're too intelligent and experienced for that. Of course, hearing that pleased me. Would it be okay if we discussed it together? You should, in my opinion, know the truth now because sex will undoubtedly play a significant role in your life.

I innocently questioned, "Everything like what?"

For one thing, "about boys and their peckers."

"Peckers?"

Yes, between their legs, you are correct.

Ah, that.

"Let's get some ice cream before continuing. We are able to converse while eating. We ate ice cream and as soon as we were seated next to one another once more, he inquired, "Have any of the males seen your breasts Celine?"

Of course not, I reply.

It's not like that's a terrible thing, you know.

They even no longer want me to participate in their game.

"I'm aware of a way to fix that. I am aware of how to convince them to allow you play.

Really? I questioned as I pushed the ice cream in more quickly.

"Sure. If you can play, promise their major guy—the one who seems to have control—that you'll let him see your breasts. After the game, you find a quiet location and show him the photos. He will respond by saying, "Hell yeah." You shouldn't touch me right now since we can discuss that later.

"Oh, I see. So you get to play with them, and all he gets is a look. I don't mean your breasts; I mean the boys.

I seem to have laughed at that. I'm not sure whether other ladies my age were as gullible, but I sure was making it simple for him.

"Celine You'll get to play ball when I show you that it will work.

CHAPTER 22

How are you, Uncle Norm?

"Take off your top and bra for me, and I'll show you the evidence," He was beginning to perspire, so it must be very warm in there. Anyway, I complied with his request and he carefully examined my breasts.

"You have some gorgeous ones, Celine."

"I'm grateful,"

"All right, now I'll show you that boys will want to be in your presence. He did so by removing his cock through the leg of his underwear.

Austin muttered, "That bastard," as Celine gasped in horror and put her palm to her mouth. James was looking at Celine to see if she was alright.

"My world was spinning, God. To me, his cock seemed enormous. Massive, extremely hard-looking, and extremely moist at the tip.

Before he said, "See Celine, seeing you made my cock so erect," he gave me some time to observe it. Those males will now respond similarly. Actually, they resemble me the most. They would enjoy seeing your tits as well as feeling their cocks expand and become this hard. Young or old like your dad and I, all males are that that. That is simply how nature created us.

I've never seen one before, Uncle Norm. It's far larger than I anticipated.

The boys you want to play ball with will have them in different sizes, but mine is very big, and they will get bigger as the males mature, he assured her. He said, "Want to know a secret? Describe that.

My cock, put your hand on it.

"Aunt Norm I don't...."

"Really, it's all right. I'll just sit here and see how one feels, and then I'll reveal my surprise to you.

I was so frightened to touch him, but he didn't move as he said, and I was forced to just stare at his firm cock instead. He appeared to be sitting there as calmly as he possibly could when I looked at him. I hesitated before making a choice, but I have to admit that I was interested as my palm lingered over him. They all smiled despite the terrible wrong that had been done to her: "I was inquisitive about so many things, and this was a significant one...sorry. "Okay, I touched it. My little hand seemed to get so much smaller as it delicately wrapped around it. Although he remained motionless and fulfilled his word, he informed me, "Sorry honey, but that's something I can't control," as his cock twitched. It occasionally does that," and I gaped. I was hesitant to touch the fluid drop that was on the tip. All I knew was that it might have been poop. When he said, "Now pull back a little and you'll see how the skin slides," I did what he said, and once again, he was correct. I was now staring at the entire, brilliantly pink head that was shimmering. He was simply grinning when I turned to face him. To me, he appeared to be my Uncle Norm from before. I was fascinated, but I also knew deep down that there was a reason I shouldn't be touching him. Actually, I was extremely inquisitive.

Celine was demonstrating her strength, but she was avoiding eye contact with everybody. The fact that she had to fight this particular battle meant that they could all only offer their support. They all wished they could do something to make it easier for her.

Verse Seventeen

When Celine finally turned to look at James, he grinned at her from below. There she was with my hand on his cock and he remarked, "While you're discovering what a cock feels like, I'll tell you a few of intriguing things," she said while exchanging a fleeting smile. Erectile tissue is what makes up a man's cock. That simply implies that despite having no bones, it can become incredibly stiff and hard. Then he touched a breast on me. He reassured me, "Honey, it's okay," and I winced. I'll demonstrate more for you. He continued to touch me and probe my entire breast, saying, "See, your nipple was already hard due to your youth more than anything, but also when your nipples are touched like this, they get harder. I was dumbfounded and perplexed. Then then, my world was spinning and I enjoyed learning about his cock and my breasts even though I knew I shouldn't have let it. "Look at how firm and brittle your nipples are. Although they now lack erectile tissue, they nevertheless have unique muscles that enable erection. Me caressing you maintains the hardness of your nipples in the same way that you playing with my cock does. You are doing fantastic work, and I appreciate everything you are doing for me. Interested in learning more? What is another crucial component of sex education?

Who or what is Uncle Norm? It didn't take me long to realize that I shouldn't have requested that, but by that time it was too late for me.

For me, honey, stand up. Place yourself directly in front of me. After following his instructions, I froze as he once more forced me to remove my shorts and underwear. Oh my God, do you guys still want me to carry on like this?

Angela stated: Celine, it's up to you. Yes, we want to hear everything if you want us to know or if it will assist you to be honest. It's possible that keeping your secret hidden under a veil of denial is actually making things worse for you. All of those negative thoughts and memories might perish from exposure if talking about it will lift that shroud. Only you have the authority to decide this." Maybe if I omit a few specifics. He fingered me after explaining about erectile tissue once more while placing his fingers between my legs. But it was enough to genuinely frighten me—not deep or hard. I was ready for it to end, yet what he was doing also felt amazing. I cried because I was so confused. As he chatted quietly till I calmed down, he picked me up and hugged me close to him. Then he added that we may learn more the next day, with the exception of one final point. At that point, he demonstrated for me how to jack him off and make him cum. Whenever God... I'm unable to even speak it. I was in awe. I stopped crying and completely forgot about being naked and his touch. The next time we spoke, he promised to elaborate on that. After he had calmed down, he warned me not to tell my mother because he didn't want her to be upset or wounded by the news. I agreed that everything would be kept a secret since he simply didn't want to damage her feelings.

So, Celine, were there any other occasions? Austin queried.

"Yes, there have been other occasions. Even when I was outside, I spent a lot of time there while naked. Dad then suddenly appeared one day not long after Mom had dropped me off. He told me I looked so special and pretty in my underwear and he was so happy to see me. I ran to him because I was happy to see him. I loved it because Dad and Uncle Norm were so kind to me and so flattering. Dad was there, but I didn't tell Mom because they warned it would be bad if she knew. I now had a new secret to guard. I couldn't help but look at Dad when I first saw him in a bikini because, to me, he reminded me so much of Uncle Norm but was a little longer. Oh god, this is getting harder," she said, wiping her eyes with a tissue. "Yes,

CHAPTER 23

Dad was just like Uncle Norm. He even had me jack him off, my own father. but then not long after that day, Dad arrived again and of course again I was naked, but this time he had two boys with him from his neighborhood and they were naked too."

That's when Celine lost control and sobbed as she turned to bury her face into James's shirt. He pulled her close to him and just held her close and let her cry as he told her, "It's okay honey, we're here and we love you. You were the victim honey and none of that was of your creation. Her left arm went around him and held on as her tears flowed and Austin and Angela joined them, comforting her as best they could.

James was still holding her close as he said, "You don't have to tell any more."

"There's more to tell."

"I'm sure there is, but give yourself a break now and catch your breath. Look up at me would you?"

She turned her head and looked up as he said, "I love you. We all love you now more than ever. How you lived through that and still turned out to be the fantastic woman you are I'll never know."

She wasn't crying, but her face was flushed and her eyes were red and her hair was a mess, but she managed a little smile before she said, "I warned you my story was going to be a downer and that I'd cry."

"But thank you for sharing that with us. I agree with Angela. I don't think it can hurt for you to talk about that. Come with me and we'll get you put back together." He walked her back to his bathroom and said, "Give me a second. He retrieved a fresh washcloth and getting it wet with very warm water, he stood close to her and with his hand on her back to help support her, he gently bathed her face and down around her neck, rinsed the cloth and did that again for her as she submitted herself to his gentle touch. Angela went back to check on them and saw what they were doing and went back to Austin.

James fished through one of the drawers and producing a hair brush, he ignored her feeble protestations and gently brushed her hair. He knew almost nothing about what he was doing, but it was for therapeutic benefit, not hairstyle. He put the brush down then and putting his arms around her he kissed her. Not deeply nor passionately, but a long gentle kiss before he said, "You are so damn incredible. So strong and so resilient. I'm so lucky to count you as my best friend."

"Thank you and thank you for taking such good care of me."

He smiled and said, "Okay my turn. Thank you for removing your bra."

She smiled and said, "Liked that did you?"

"Very much, but I don't know how or when you did that."

Celine turned a little and pulled it from under the sink and showed him with a smile.

"Angela didn't think that was the right thing to do. She was afraid that I was polluting or changing our close knit group of four."

James smiled and said, "In my humble opinion, you've improved our little close knit group of four by about tenfold."

She kissed him quickly and said, "Thank you hon. Now we better get out there before they decide we're doing something indecent."

"Honey, with you it would never be indecent, it would be spectacular."

"Oh honey, Angela was right, our little group is changing and changing fast." She led the way and made it as far as the bathroom doorway before she stopped and told him, "James...I loved feeling your hands on me and I liked the idea that I was so vulnerable to your touch. That there was nothing to stop you from touching my breasts."

"Except you," James added as they went out. They were entering the living room when Celine told James, "Maybe, maybe not," and she smiled and sat down on the love seat. James wanted her to explain that, but it was too late for anymore private conversation.

"You look about a hundred percent better," Austin told her.

"Thanks, I just needed time to collect myself and freshen up." She shifted a little then and told them, "I'm sorry for spoiling the rest of our evening."

CHAPTER 24

"You didn't spoil it," Austin told her. We are in this together and we don't have to be laughing or entertaining each other just because we're together. We are here for you just as you are here for any of us. You've been carrying one hell of a burden all alone, and if telling us about that helps you even a little it's worth it and more. And if you need to talk more we're here for you. Anytime of day or night."

"Thank you Austin and I mean that. This is why it's so great for us to have our little safe time together. There's no other way I could have opened up like that. Only to you three and only here. This has helped me more than all of those sessions with my therapist did after that nightmare was over."

"Celine," Angela said, "Can I ask you a question or would you rather I not?"

"I don't mind, ask me."

"Well I wanted to know about what happened with...or rather to those boys, but instead I'll ask you what happened to your dad and uncle?"

"I'll tell all of you about the two boys, that I only knew as Chuck and Marty, some day. As to my dad and uncle, Dad is still in prison. You see, after that last experience I told Mom everything, and I do mean everything. God I thought she would lose her mind before it was over. But she was strong enough to call the police right then."

"You're dad is in prison? I thought he was dead."

"He is as far as I'm concerned. He's eligible for parole in a few years and then I don't know what will happen to him. Needless to say, he can never be close to kids again and his record will chase him forever."

"And your uncle, the one that to me was, of the two, the worst thing alive."

"The father of one of those boys caught him and beat him so badly that he wasn't expected to live. He was after Dad, but missed him, so Uncle Norm was his second choice. Old Uncle had so many fractures that I can't remember them all. He was paralyzed from the neck down, lost an eye and I don't know what all. There was brain damage, but I don't remember the details. He died a couple of years after he went to prison."

"Too bad, I think prison life in his condition would have been worse than death. What happened to the boys father that beat your uncle?"

"Sad to say, he had to spend some time in prison, but not much. I don't remember the details. There were a whole lot of people that saw him as a hero and a loving father. Okay, I promise that from now on, if I have any stories to share, they will be much more upbeat."

James told her, "You just promise to be here for the next time and we'll listen to your stories no matter if they are funny or tragic, though I can't imagine one any worse than what you shared this time."

It was time for the evening to end, and one by one they left. Austin was first and then Celine and she and Angela shared a long hug and whispers. Then after Celine left, Angela helped James pick up the empty beer bottles and the kitchen and then said, "I'm going home now."

"Angela, thanks for the help."

"Thank you very much."

He walked with her to the door and they too shared a long firm hug before he looked at her and said, "You my love are one special lady."

She blinked and said, "Thank you."

"Angela, why the tears?"

"It's nothing...really."

"Please tell me, it's not like you to be like this."

"I'm okay really. I guess it was Celine's story. It was all so very tragic and sick. How can she be normal even now?"

"Because she's strong and refuses to have her whole life destroyed by her so called father and uncle. Sure you won't stay long enough for us to talk honey?"

"No, I'll be okay."

"Remember, we share the bad and the good. There isn't much I don't know about you or you about me. You've seen me throwing up and you've seen me have a temper tantrum. I've seen you so green and sick you scared me. I've held you close after what's his name broke up with you. I'm here for you."

"I know and thanks, but really I'm okay. I just need some sleep I think."

"Okay, but you know how to get hold of me, anytime day or night. Or Celine or Austin for that matter."

"I know. Night James."

"Night Angela."

For Celine, Austin's story about adolescent love and exploration was sweet and normal and erotic, where her experience went from not feeling right to being scary and then to feeling violated. For a while it had been difficult for her to listen to Austin's story, but it didn't involve adults so she was able to get past that and thoroughly enjoy and visit Austin's experiences. Maybe he helped her to face some facts and to put the negative in her past away and focus on the positives in her past. Then she realized that at least to some extent, bringing her story of her horrible nightmare to light really had helped her. It was still there and always would be, but that time in her life seemed to weigh less. The more she thought about it, the more she was glad that she had opened up and shared her nightmare with her friends.

Angela's night after hearing Celine's story was at best a restless one. She kept seeing James touching and caressing Celine, and seeing him tenderly tending to her in the bathroom. What the two of them were feeling was pretty obvious to her and that made her cry again. Damn it, she thought, why is James determined to destroy their safe times together? She hurt, but she couldn't very well go to Celine or James with her thoughts and concerns. She waited until almost noon Sunday to call Austin and told him she needed to talk to him. He was there within half an hour and they shared a long hug as he asked her, "What's wrong Angela?"

"I'm scared Austin," and she started to softly cry.

"Come with me," and he led her to the couch where they sat down, him with his back tucked into the pocket formed by the large armrest and the back and her tucked into him with his arm around her and the side of her face resting on his chest. Her right arm went around him loosely and he said, "Tell me what's wrong Angela? How can I help you?"

"Damn it Austin, I told James not long ago that our little group was changing and it is. Austin I don't want to see that happen. I don't want us to lose our times together."

"How do you see it changing? What's so different that it causes you so much hurt?"

"Didn't you watch James and Celine last night? Didn't you see him all but put his hand on her breasts and...and how he would hold her close. Austin, Celine took her bra off in the bathroom even before she started her story. He...his hand was all over her back and front."

CHAPTER 25

"Yeah I did notice that, what else?"

"What else? What more does there need to be to prove my point? Okay, he took her to the bathroom and bathed her. He bathed her Austin, and...I don't know what all, but they were in there a long time together. Damn it there's something big going on between them."

"I see what you're saying. Okay, let's say there is something between them, why is that a death sentence for our foursome?"

"Because the whole dynamic will change."

"I'm not sure I follow your reasoning, but there's another way to look at it. I agree that we are changing. I can see it in our body language. Not just James and Celine's, but also yours and mine. Each of us is evolving. But Angela, that doesn't have to mean the end of us getting together like we have for so long."

"Wait, you said I was changing, how? How am I changing?"

"You're maturing just as all of us are. There was a book published a number of years ago that I ran across one day. The title was something like, change is inevitable but growth is optional. We are changing, but it's up to us to decide what to do with that fact. Do we do something about it? Do we try to adjust? Or do we let what we have slowly wither and die?"

"You're just saying make lemonade out of the lemons."

"That's right. If it's as important to the four of us as I'm sure it is, we'll find a way to adapt and continue."

"When we met Kelly that night I saw that as a sign of change."

"I'm not sure about that one. I think James was just visiting his past one last time. We all have points in our lives where we would like to go back and savor those times again. James was lucky enough to do a version of that."

"Do you think he and Kelly made love again?"

"He denied it, but yes I think they did. Why do I think that? I don't know actually and I guess it doesn't really matter. He stepped back in time and now he's back where he belongs."

"So you don't see him continuing with her?"

"Nah. Oh, she was a looker for her age without a doubt, but they had about as much in common as a cat and a dog have. Angela can I be truly honest? It will probably hurt your feelings."

"Yes, of course you can, that's what I want."

"I'm not sure any of us ever want that, but okay. I think you're making more out of this than is really there."

"I don't think so, but go ahead."

"I agree, James and Celine were in the bathroom for a long time, but that reminds me of the time James spent a good part of a night nursing you through the flu. He held you and wiped your forehead with a cool cloth. He watched you throw up and he'd kiss you lightly a minute later. Remember that time Angela?"

Her voice had dropped to a near whisper as she answered, "Yes, I remember that."

"Do you see that as being different?"

"I don't know, but somehow...yes I do. I can't explain it I guess. There was something different going on between them."

"Did you feel like James loved you even as you barfed?"

"Of course he did, and you would have done the same for me."

"That's right. It's only my opinion, but I think James's love for Celine was what you were seeing. I'll go a step farther and agree that it may have been a little different, simply because of us evolving, maturing as I mentioned earlier. Honey, I'm no wiser than you or the others are, but I'm trying to look at things from a different angle is all. Your fears are real and not without foundation, but it's up to us how we deal with it in the future. Maybe talk to James about it too and tell him how worried you are."

"I have to think about that one, but thanks. I'll be okay now."

"Are you sure? I don't want to leave you here when you're still sad and worried and confused."

"I'm okay. I am still worried, but I want to think about what you've said. About how you see things. Maybe I do need to think about accepting change and stop trying to prevent it."

"Exactly. We can't stop it and trying to do that will only cause us pain and disappointment that failure brings. That can't be an option for us."

They were walking toward the door as Angela said, "I'm okay now and thank you for racing over here."

"Anytime and you know that."

"I do know that, and that's exactly what we have to fight to preserve. Bye Austin." Before he could get far she added, "Love you Austin."

"Love you too Angela," and he left.

Thursday after work, Austin called James and went over to see him. "Grab a beer," James said as he rinsed his hands in the kitchen sink. Austin grabbed two and sat at the table. James joined him and said, "So what's up?"

"Angela called me last Sunday and needed to talk to me so I went over and caught her crying. Or at least she had been."

"She cried before she left Saturday night too, what the hell is wrong? She wouldn't tell me anything."

"Well I'm not sure either, but I'll tell you what I think." He took time to sample his beer and then putting the sweating bottle on the table again said, "She seemed very upset about how you were with Celine last Saturday night."

"What did I do?"

"That was my question to her basically. She saw you tending to Celine and...in Angela' words now...running your hand all over her."

CHAPTER 26

James laughed and said, "Yeah damn that Celine left her bra in the bathroom for some reason. She teased the hell out of me."

"I know, Angela told me all about that believe me. She says that's proof that our foursome is changing and she doesn't like that idea."

"It is changing and Celine made the same comment to me. But so what? We all change, but that doesn't mean we have to stop getting together."

"I don't think you're picking up on how stressed Angela is over all of that. I reminded her that you were just seeing to Celine when she needed somebody to hold her and tended to her needs. Just like you did for her when she was sick."

"And you did for her when she got so drunk that night."

"Right. Anyway, we talked and when I left her she seemed a little better, but not great. James either she's making more out of this than she should, or you and Celine really do have a thing started."

"Austin, I'll admit that I got a little carried away with her, but damn it I didn't plan it like that. She had my heart melting for her as she revealed her nightmare."

"One thing I think is, Celine's story was a real tipping point for the four of us. I think listening to her affected all of our emotions and probably Angela's the most. Why I'm not sure, but she seemed to really be affected by that night. Celine's revealing her dark and terrible secret helped her a lot. I really believe that James, I think that us knowing about her father and uncle and that whole scene was really cathartic for her. I think she left feeling somewhat relieved of that burden and maybe cleansed in a way. Her horrible experience no longer had to be hidden. I think she was carrying a certain amount of guilt around. Why she would I don't know, but that's what I think. Anyway, she really benefited from telling us. I know you were affected by it and that shows by how you tended to her. I think you could have cried for her in fact, but you held that inside of you. I know I shed a couple of tears for her. I'll even go a little farther and say that her story will turn out to have a positive affect on us. I think it will help us move on and evolve in a way. As adults and as friends."

"You've really been thinking about this."

"Almost constantly. Angela seemed so damn rattled. Out of proportion to what the situation called for in fact. I don't...oh shit."

"What?"

"She's jealous of Celine."

"Nah, that can't be it Austin, she's seen me tease Celine, kiss her and I don't know what all. She knows I love Celine and..."

"None of that matters. What you're talking about is past. Remember, we're all changing. Our emotions were kicked around like an old soccer ball last Saturday night. We went from my story of erotica, childhood discovery and all of those simple and sweet emotions, to the hell of child abuse and sick adults. Damn what a switch that was. I think all of that added to emotions for all of us. You didn't need any help with your emotions involving Celine, and with all of that added, looking back anyway, I'm about half surprised you two didn't make love. Anyway, I have to wonder if that didn't kick Angela's emotions and force her to realize something. That something being she has stronger feelings for you than she knew or even wants to admit maybe. Look, I could be wrong, but the pieces fit."

"Aw shit, Austin that can't be right."

"Are you saying that you don't or can't feel that way for her? Is this going to be a deal breaker for you two?" "Oh hell no, but...shit, I need some time to think about this. Damn it man, you just might be right. She was over here not long ago and we had a great evening together. I mean we didn't make love, but we really did have a great time. I was even thinking about asking her back so we could have an evening together again."

"Great. Of course she may say no, but go for it. Maybe you can figure out if there's anything to my suspicions."

"Yeah I think you're right. How would you feel if Angela and I were to get together as a couple?"

"I think that would be awesome."

"And Celine?"

"No, you can't have both of him." Then before James could say anything Austin said, "Hell, I don't know, but I can't imagine she'd object at all. Well other than that would mean you couldn't have your hands all over her again."

James smiled and said, "And that would be a loss."

"Oh yeah, we're all changing like the seasons, only a whole lot faster."

"Don't say anything to Celine okay? I mean this could still go about any direction."

"I'll keep it to myself. We could both be wrong that's for sure. Good luck figuring it out, and I hope you don't make her mad if it turns out we were off base with our thinking."

Gee, I appreciate that idea.

Austin raised himself and tipped his beer back. Good luck deciding where your future lays, my man.

"Yeah. There is no pressure.

James did consider Angela and everything they had in common. He grinned as he recalled the two of them stripping off when they were young to compare their differences. He touched her where her half was missing, and she felt his small cock. At his birthday party, he recalled their first kiss. He simply lay on the couch and soaked in the memories as they poured in. Angela seemed to be more involved in his history than everyone else.

CHAPTER 27

That, however, did not assist him in the present or the future. After giving up, he dialed her number. Hello, I'm here.

"Hi James, What are you working on?

Tomorrow night, I was considering taking you to Cabrera's for pizza and drinks, and then we could spend the rest of the evening here talking.

That sounds fantastic. James wasn't sure what to make of Angela's voice because it was just like she used to sound. However, spending the evening with her would be wonderful whatsoever, so he decided to enjoy it and let any problems naturally arise. Then, he would decide what to think or say.

Through supper, they remained cheerful and in good spirits. They laughed together and discussed a variety of topics, but not Celine and her tale. In actuality, they made no mention of last Saturday night. They were quite quiet as James drove them back to his house, and they stayed that way as they entered. He dragged Angela along with him as he sat down on the couch, kicked off his shoes, and propped his feet up on the coffee table when she declined any further drinks. You know, Austin's tale last night was fantastic," James remarked. Everything seemed so natural and innocent in its own way. Many young people have had intense crushes on relatives or other people. It was also quite sexy.

It really was and was very nice, Angela replied while grinning at him. I was taken aback by how long he continued to hold the candle for her. It usually only happens once, followed by a little period of reliving it, and then it vanishes.

"He didn't go into details, but it did seem to go on for a while. I could almost picture it occurring when he described them gently stripping while heading down the ancient cow path.

I'll bet you wish you had a memory like that, or did you, she continued, grinning once more.

"No, not at all. How about you?"

"Not only me. I doubt I could have performed the same actions as his Sandra Grahams. I was somewhat timid back then.

"were friendly and willing to participate in activities."

I guess you're correct, but I wouldn't have had the confidence back then to undress in front of you, Austin, or any of the neighborhood youngsters, she acknowledged with a smile.

And this?

Before replying, "You know what I mean," she gave him a beaming face as she hit him.

"Angela, have you ever questioned why, out of all the kids in our neighborhood, it has only been the four of us who have remained so close over the years?

"I do consider that, but only because we are so similar. that we share the same values and opinions regarding certain topics.

Even Celine's ex-husband couldn't separate us. Austin's presently unsuccessful engagement didn't even slow us down. Austin may have been completely off base. As usual, the two of them were making jokes and making fun of each other. She exuded happiness and ease. But even as they conversed, he was thinking about what he and Austin had discussed. He also had to confess how wonderful it felt to have her all to himself and snuggled up against him. He put Celine in her place in his head, which of course made sense, but he and Angela shared a deeper link. He had no idea why, but upon reflection, he realized that it had always been that way. When it came to the four of them, she was always the one on his thoughts first.

He made his choice while she was using the restroom. He was going to accomplish what he had planned to do and then proceed from there. He had to figure out why she had sobbed that night and then again with Austin, that much was certain.

He caught her as soon as she exited the restroom and embraced her. He held her while lowering his lips to hers as she stared up at him, bringing his hands up to either side of her face. Just as his tongue entered between her lips and she gave him another kiss, Angela's hands reached out to his arms. "James, never kiss me like that again, unless you mean it," she commanded as she gently pulled back just enough for him to look into her eyes. Unless there is more to it than just a long-standing friendship. Again, he kissed her. She responded to it just as passionately and for as long as she had before. Oh my God, James, let's stop. We need to discuss things.

What would you like to discuss?

Why did you kiss me in such a way?

"Why else, besides the fact that I wanted to"

But how can you treat me like this when you came so close to kissing Celine on Saturday night?

With one exception, Angela, I didn't even approach becoming intimate with Celine. I will admit that I came close to caressing her breasts. Once I realized she wasn't wearing a bra, yes, I really did want to. However, aside from that, I was with her just as I frequently have been with you. I felt a connection to her and love for her, just like I had for you ever since we were young.

But it was a friendship, not desire, that you felt for me.

That's accurate, and once more, I felt the same way about Celine.

"So, are you suggesting that we are on the same page and that you have kissed or will kiss Celine the same way that you just kissed me?"

That's not the case. Telling you that, that was how I used to be. Angela, it's different now. We've all changed, but I think I've changed the most.

CHAPTER 28

But James, you can't have both of us, damn it.

"Angela, I'm not attempting to have both of you. It was actually you that I just kissed, not Celine, but twice in fact. I love you very much, Angela.

She started crying now. James, please stop saying those things, damn you.

Even if they're accurate, Austin was here the other night, and after our lengthy conversation about a wide range of topics, I've been thinking about the four of us as well as about you and me. Your crying on Saturday night kept me up at night. And here you are crying once more. Tell me it's because your affections for me have intensified, please.

"Damn James, I'm so confused. Okay, I'll admit that I've grown afraid of you.

"I propose that we celebrate rather than be afraid."

"You know it's not that easy, yet it's not. What transpires at our Saturday night get-togethers? What has happened to Celine and you?

"First off, I don't understand why that should have any bearing at all on our get-togethers. In that regard, nothing alters. I'll continue to be very honest and open, and I'll divulge information that I'd never share with anyone else. I'll adore you all. When the four of us are together, the only thing I want to change is for the better. Now, I have to say something about

Celine. Angela, you are aware of my love for her. Without hesitation, I would do anything for her. She is the most significant person in my life after you.

"Nearby me?"

"Yes, next to you," he said as he gave her another kiss as she was still sobbing.

"What the heck, honey? What else is causing you trouble? How may I be of assistance to you?

"Hold on tight, honey. Don't let go; hold me. Oh my gosh, I hope the others understand, she whispered as he wrapped his arms around her and she held him close.

"I believe Austin is aware,"

What exactly did you tell him?

"He told me everything; I said nothing. He may have seen the battle you were fighting, and I believe he looked right through me when I was speaking. Tell me, what will it do to you if I hold Celine the next time, kiss her, and tell her I love her?

I'll be fine, but if you ever touch her tits by reaching under her blouse, we're going to argue.

Even if it only occurs once? he asked with a smile.

He grinned in return, and she responded, "Yes, even then. You can tell her you love her and give her a kiss, but I better never catch her gagging on your tongue.

"Then I'll remain shallow." Despite her smile, she struck him.

Angela, I'll tell you this straight up. I won't ever make out with her. We have a strong link because of our complete transparency and honesty, thus I'll never do anything behind your back either. Even if someone's feelings are wounded, I never wish to keep a secret from you or the other people.

Then, after giving him a kiss, she remarked, "So does this complete openness and honesty involve telling them about us having sexual relations?"

Sure, as it hasn't occurred.

"And once it has done?"

"We must then inform everyone of the situation. even how frequently and how often you orgasm."

"No, you won't. The answer is no.

"We can discuss that,"

Yes, like your current lover.

"No, when we've worn each other out," he replied as he drew her toward the bedroom. Before we can divulge all the juicy facts, we first need to get to know one another.

As they walked down the hallway toward his bedroom, she said, "You bet we have to talk about that," but she was also grinning.

When they next got together on a Saturday night, Angela and James kept their relationship a secret, although she was always at his house and arrived much earlier than the others.

CHAPTER 29

Austin and Celine arrived almost simultaneously, and the four of them were quickly seated in the living room with iced tea this time.

"I have a new tale to share. It's brief and unlike the previous one.

Austin gushed, "Fantastic." Alright, let's settle in. As Celine started her narrative, Angela swiftly shifted to the floor between James's legs and settled in.

"This incident occurred a while back. I was probably around 19 years old at the time. Of course, this was before I got married. Anyhow, I left Maria Scout house and headed for my flat on Claremont Circle. Even though it was extremely late and dark, I had frequently traveled the same route at that hour because the area was so calm, safe, and serene. I don't believe it was more than eight blocks, but anyway, I liked it in the wonderful weather. Anyway, after traveling three or four blocks, I thought I heard something. It sounded like somebody was brushing a shrub. I halted before moving on. Then I heard what sounded like a branch snapping. Once more, I paused and peered about, but the place was empty and eerily quiet. There was enough light for strolling, but it was far from bright enough to truly illuminate the neighborhood because of how far apart and weak the street lights were. The next snap was heard by me. like the sound of a tiny stick. I was now becoming frightened. I coerced myself to walk, though admittedly at a faster speed, because I knew that if I started to run, it would only fuel my concerns and cause me to panic.

God, I'm getting goose flesh listening to this, Angela stroked her forearm and exclaimed.

"When I heard more snapping, I was seriously pondering my alternatives. I couldn't pinpoint its exact origin because it was coming from behind me. I continued for another few streets or so before I heard a loud snap, which caused me to turn around once more. Then, from behind me, someone ran up and flung their arms around me, placing their hands on my breasts. I screamed pretty loudly when he was holding firmly with two hands full. My a$$hole boyfriend Leo came out and started laughing at me. He found everything about it to be really hilarious. No one has ever been as irate as I was, I assure you. I yelled at Leo while ripping Dale's hands from my breasts, then I turned on Dale and called him every four-letter word I could think of, including ones I made up. I was so furious that I spat. Leo followed Dale out the door while making excuses in between spasms of laughter. Then I turned on him and threatened to cut off Dale's hands at the wrists if he ever touched me again, and I warned Leo that I would shout "rape" if he did. Both of them were never seen by me again. That is my narrative.

CHAPTER 30

Celine, I swear I felt your dread and then your rage. If I had been there, I would have assisted you in chopping off Dale's hands and then Leo's pecker. They both chuckled at it and then got up to get their custo Sandra beers.

Angela stated, "When we go back in, I have something to say...well, confess maybe and tell," as they were enjoying their beverages in the kitchen.

Austin exclaimed, "Hot damn," and inquired, "Is it a juicy story?"

It might be, but I haven't had a drink enough.

Celine simply smiled when James made eye contact with her, grinned, and retrieved four more beers from the fridge with the words "Let's go swap stories."

When Angela noticed that James was sitting on the floor this time, she grinned and laid on her back with her head resting on his leg. Even before she could start speaking, James's hand was already tucked inside her baggy shirt. She knew exactly what she wanted to happen, but she didn't want to give James any coaching beforehand. He aced what amounted to a test and did so with flying colors.

"All right, first a confession, and Austin, this will sort of explain my strange behavior lately. Celine, do you recall how I persuaded you to lie like I am doing right now with your head resting on James's thigh the last time we were here?

"I clearly recall it, but I never expressed gratitude for it."

"Thanks for asking. James thoroughly enjoying the encounter was something I hadn't anticipated. Yes, it is incorrect. I didn't anticipate how much it would bother me. When you finished telling your story, I was practically crying for you. Okay, let's fast-forward until after your back has been massaged from butt to neck.

"Yes, and once more, thank you, Angela. I hope to receive that treat shortly.

Then, while you were lying on your back, James's hand teased you from your waistline to, shall we say, well up your belly, without making any further comments.

I wasn't wearing a bra up to my boobs, but that's okay, Angela.

"All right, thanks."

Angela looked up at James, who was smiling down at her and teasing her with his thumb running over the bottom of her bra. James was holding her hand just below her breasts.

Okay, so we departed, and I'll save certain details for later, but I won't keep anything a secret. The other night, James offered me to join him for dinner and drinks, after which we went back to his house to discuss. That conversation eventually grew longer and more serious, at which point I became enraged with him. He told me how much he loves you, Celine, and how he would sacrifice anything for you. But shortly before that, he gave me an extremely passionate kiss. You see, Jamess was experiencing some tension at the time. Naturally, we spoke at length. Then, well, Celine is back. James acknowledged that he really wanted to continue worshiping your breasts when his hand was that close to them, but doing that in front of Austin and I would have been really nasty.

Austin grinned and replied, "Tacky hell." It would have been fantastic.

Austin honey, we all need to talk about how you're changing, Celine remarked as she sat down on the floor between his legs. Everyone here needs to enter your wicked little head.

You might regret it, he said.

As Angela continued, "Anyway," she sensed James's fingertips slipping down under her breast. Anyway, we resolved the issue and then kissed once more, or maybe we kissed and then, whatever. I will be staying all night tonight even though James hasn't yet discovered that I have been at his house every night this week. Her bra was pushed up and out of the way as he proceeded to tickle her breasts as she glanced up at him and smiled.

How serious is this development, Austin questioned, looking first at James and then at Angela.

Angela remarked, "We're still working on that, but it's pretty serious," as James shrugged and grinned.

When Celine stood up, she asked James if his whisky was in its normal spot.

It is; please assist yourself.

"Thank you; I believe I will. It is necessary to do something unusual on this occasion.

Celine grinned as she put her hand on Angela's almost-exposed breasts as she followed her to the kitchen. It appears that you are copying my strategy, in my opinion.

"Fire against fire. Celine, James talked a lot about you. Not only about his nearly touching you, but also about how much he loves you and everything else. I was beginning to feel envious once more. He was desperate to touch your breasts.

For the record, Angela, I really wanted him to do it as well.

Even in front of Austin and I, perhaps?

"Yes, even in front of Austin and you. He was truly igniting my passion.

"I know he can do that. Just for the record, Celine, I don't mind.

"Wait. Does it not bother you if he touches my breasts?

I warned him not to make love to you or there would be conflict.

If I were in your position, I would have said that I would cut off his cock.

There are no secrets, therefore I can say that he too has a really great one.

Oh, that's excellent. Thank you for teaching me that.

We both realize that day will come when you'll witness it.

I don't think so.

You never know, there are both yours and his birthday and Christmas presents to consider.

What happened to Angela, who was envious?

"I felt at ease once he told me he really loved me. We are changing rapidly, as you mentioned, and perhaps I am changing the most.

THE END